A ROBIN WAITS

SHORT FICTION

KIRK WARD ROBINSON

HIGHLAND
HOME

Nashville, Tennessee

A Robin Waits
Short Fiction

A HIGHLAND EDITION

Amanda Valentine, Editor

Designed by Victoria Valentine
PageandCoverDesign.com

Printed in the United States of America

HighlandHome Publishing
Nashville, Tennessee
37215

ISBN 10: 0-9996042-7-9
ISBN 13: 978-0-9996042-7-4

Visit www.kirkwardrobinson.com

Be still yon worlds

a-venturing near.

Sage time doth echo

that ye may hear.

CONTENTS

OF SALT AND SORROW

BRUSSARD LEANED WEARILY on his rake as thunder boomed beyond the northern hills. Menacing clouds were piling against the higher reaches, cutting a dark diagonal across an otherwise inspiring sky. A more worrying thought was that what he heard might not be thunder at all, but the big guns coming closer. If so, their proximity would be unsettling although far from unnerving. The northern hills were high and unyielding, still mottled with snow in places. They had held back hordes for centuries, and would certainly do so again.

He knelt to yank a cluster of prickly weeds from the base of a lichen-encrusted apple tree, then looked up with a sigh at the dozens of other apple trees—arranged in rows like ancient ruins—that required the same service. Farther down the line grew the plums, and beyond these the quince, the figs, the pears and the peaches, each grove its own place, its own country with its own needs. It was too much work for one old man, and yet these had all been planted by one old man, distant Hector, a grandfather's grandfather who resided so far back in Brussard's lineage that no likeness of Hector, no scrawled note, no relic whatsoever remained of him except this orchard.

Brussard stood with a grunt and a creaking knee and continued to rake at the brown, leathery leaves at his feet. It was mightily hot for so early in the spring, and had remained unseasonably warm deep into last fall, luring the trees into continued growth when they should have been preparing themselves for winter. The first freeze of fall came late, a day after he had actually worked shirtless and dripping in the unyielding sun, and this had fixed the leaves to the trees in shrouds of ugly brown that held on throughout the shortened winter. He'd never seen anything like it in his long years, this traitorous weather, once so contentedly consistent in his sheltered valley and now so inexplicably unpredictable. Others talked of it, but their words were foolish, based on the heretical pronouncement that people themselves had caused this to happen, as if people could somehow reach into the sky and change the very fundament of the seasons! He laughed at the folly of such claims.

Still, he had no explanation for it, no prayer to offer in remedy, and no way of anticipating what the next season would bring. Now, as swollen buds pushed out new growth, the leaves had fallen at last and he must do the temperate work of fall in this sultry spring, raking and mulching the leaves so that he could feed them back into the soil.

His knuckles throbbed, and he noticed bleakly how his old, knotty hands so closely resembled the gnarled limbs that spread out above him. He hadn't pruned those limbs in two seasons, not since his sons had gone off to war, and now the limbs were wild with skeletal sprouts canting at all angles, piercing the carefully manicured umbrellas of the canopies like a Spartan army on the march. The trees were beginning to look irresponsibly unkempt, but though this stabbed him with shame the trees would still make fruit, and that fruit would still taste sweet.

Another rumble sounded beyond the hills, layered thunder that echoed concussively off the sky. It must be the war, he thought. A storm of a different kind.

He supported the war. He had pounded for it. Perceived slights had gained the irrevocable weight and momentum of a steep mountain drift. "*There must be war!*" had been cried below angry fists thrust toward azure skies, echoing in the canyons of the capital and then far and wide. Brussard had chanted with them. Even though he lived in a remote valley far from the capital, this soil, too, demanded justice, a demand that had bristled at the northern frontier with raging belligerence.

And so the first round had let loose, and then the second, followed by an orgy of violence that roused passions further still. The bombs fell, but always far away. It was his patriotic duty to send his sons into that cauldron, to repudiate the enemy even from this placid place—especially from this placid place—which had not suffered war during the lives of anyone in memory, while elsewhere in the country his fellow citizens had been forced to endure decades of depravity and indignity.

He settled against a tree to rest in the speckled shade. The distant thunder had scattered the birds. That would be good for the fruit at least, but he missed their song just the same. The floor of the orchard was also growing wild, but in a soft, velvety green way, springy under his feet and cool against his skin. He took in a pure sky that belied conflict and malice.

His country would be victorious, it must. It was written in the soil, in the rocks, in these hardy old trees themselves. Defeat was unimaginable. He was a patriot, he had done his duty, and yet he was also alone—old hands, old knees, daughters scattered with their new husbands to places beyond the hills that he had never seen, his wife gone from either heartache or heart attack and now lying with his fathers in the cemetery beyond the orchard.

He completed his work in the apple orchard well before the sun met its zenith. His stomach growled, but there would be plenty of time to eat during the gloaming hours, when he could put away his work for the day. He went to fetch his scythe, for the deepening grass must be tended. The pruning would have to wait. The hills rose in a tawny wall toward the darkening sky. Perhaps his sons were even now over those hills, doing their duty or perhaps even looking down on him as he bent to his work once more. It was best to banish such unseemly thoughts. If his sons lived, then they were fighting for victory and had no time to spare for affectionate glances homeward.

He swung his scythe, back and forth, back and forth, feeling every sweep of its cut as an ache deep in his shoulder. He remembered his father doing this same work, and vaguely, like a gauzy glimpse through a keyhole, his grandfather as well. The orchard went from father to son. For generations it had been this way, and now it was his time and his sons were off to war.

Those thoughts weighed heavily as he scythed a pathway through the center of the orchard. Providence would provide, he reassured himself. The orchard was as eternal as the land, the work endless although often rewarding, affectionate even, a loving thing. His sons would return with victory grasped tightly in their fists, the tradition would continue as it must, and then he could go to rest with his fathers.

A plume of dust traced a line along the base of the hills. This had also been a dry spring, which portended poorly for the months ahead. Presently the plume veered his way, and he watched as a battered pickup truck pounded the desiccated dust toward him. He knew the truck. It slid to a crunching halt in front of the house, and Brussard went to meet it.

"Raymonde," Brussard beamed. Raymonde was a thin man with dark eyes, and not much older than Brussard's sons.

Raymonde kicked open the creaking door and stepped out into the dust. "Brussard. You are well?"

"Yes. Tending the orchard, of course."

"Of course."

Raymonde seemed subdued, and this left Brussard a little uneasy. "What have you got there?" Brussard asked. The bed was sagging on its springs and loaded high with large, white linen bags that shed dust in the small breeze.

"Come help me with these," Raymonde said curtly, as if short of time.

Brussard's brow wrinkled. "Help you with what?"

"Help me unload a few of these bags. They're heavy and I'm tired."

Sweat ran in skeins through a glittering white powder on Raymonde's sun-browned arms. There were patches of white on his cheeks and in his hair as well.

"What is that?" Brussard asked in puzzlement.

"Stings like bloody hell is what it is," Raymonde spat back.

The content of the bags was a mystery compounded by Raymonde's peculiar behavior, but answers would come in their own time. Brussard grabbed the ear of a bag, Raymonde the other, and the two tugged until the bag plomped onto the ground with the weight of wet sand.

"Heavy," Brussard commented.

"They would be then, wouldn't they?"

"I don't understand."

"You will. Help me get another one out."

They tugged two more bags out of the bed of the truck, which rose on its springs slightly. The three bags looked like fattened pigs lying in the dust. Another round of thunder hammered the hills, shifting the fine dust on the pickup's hood.

"They're coming closer," Raymonde whispered darkly.

"It's the war, isn't it?" Brussard asked, knowing the answer but suddenly desperate for confirmation.

Raymonde gave him a gallows look. "Yes."

"Hmm." Brussard scratched his bristly gray chin. "I was just thinking that my sons might be up there right now, doing their duty."

"Your sons aren't up there."

"How can you know?"

Raymonde's face went feral. "Because nothing's left up there! At least nothing alive."

Those words were icy fingers around Brussard's heart. "What do you mean?" he asked with a quiver.

"I mean—" Raymonde slammed a fist into his truck, leaving a dent that looked no different from the others except that this one was cleaner. He turned angrily on Brussard. "I mean, Brussard, that we have lost the war. It's over, I tell you. *Over!*"

Brussard tottered back, incomprehension draining his color. "No, it can't be," he muttered in disbelief.

"It can and it is." Raymonde spilled tears that ran clownishly through the powder on his cheeks. He knuckled roughly at his eyes. "Damn, this stuff stings like hell."

Brussard was still a muddle of confusion. "No!" he exclaimed, mostly to himself. "Our Great Army cannot lose. They will beat the enemy back. They must!"

Raymonde took Brussard by the shoulders and shook the man hard. "Listen, old man. Listen! It's lost, I tell you. The enemy will be here anon, by nightfall or morning latest."

"No, no..." Brussard wrenched away from Raymonde and stumbled to his knees. "They are pigs," he muttered. "They cannot stand and fight."

"They have beaten us, old man. Accept it. We've been ordered out. We're to leave them nothing. Do you hear? Nothing."

"I don't understand."

"Burn your house and your tool shed. Burn everything. These are bags of salt. You are to sow it into the soil of your orchard. The pigs may have beat us, but they cannot *have* us."

The horror of it seeped in slowly, but then prised a pathway and followed in a flood. "Burn my house?" Brussard looked up in anguish. "Kill the *orchard?*"

"Those are your orders, Brussard. Afterward you could flee, or meet us in the southern passes withal. We will make our last stand there."

"But..."

Raymonde was scrambling back into his truck. "You're a patriot, aren't you?" he spat. "Then do your duty. Now I've been here too long." He glanced at his filthy wrist as if it held a watch. "There's no time. I have to go."

The truck spun dust in curtains as Raymonde pulled out, steering away from the hills and toward the next farm.

Brussard rose with the weary weight of despair, the dust settling on his shoulders, his nose, his lips. He ground it between his teeth, spat it at the far hills. Salting the orchard was unthinkable, but he must do his duty, mustn't he? What was he without the orchard, though, without the work that never seemed to end, and without sons who—

Could it be true? Could his sons be gone forever?

Duty was everything. What then was his duty? His duty was to see the orchard safely to the next generation. But that generation might no longer exist. A tear found a track down his weathered cheek. There was also his duty to his country, which had lost its land but not its spirit. He must do as ordered and deny the bounty of this land to the enemy. It was his only recourse. There could be no question.

He slumped to his work, his decision made by fate and lashing at him as his scythe lashed at the wildness that had grown around him. He worked late into the dusky hours, raking, scything, an eye always on the hills and what avalanche of disaster might soon spill over them. There would be no time now for the pruning. Still, the orchard looked good, not its best but still an island of serene green in the fearsome dust of a deadly spring. The enemy would never know the peace of this place. They might see it from high as a far oasis. They might acknowledge the pride, the craft, and long for its cool shade. They might even wonder who had made such a garden, but they would never have their answer, only that someone had shown love to this place; and before they could claim that love for themselves the blossoms would fall like pink snow, the leaves would wither, and soon the orchard would stand as brown as the hills.

At last it was time for the salt, which stung the fine cuts on his hands as he scooped it into a wheelbarrow. The sun was low on a purple horizon. The storm clouds had dissipated in the heat of day, and the hills were now lit in soft evening shades. The thunder had not sounded for some hours. He levered the heavily laden wheelbarrow to the foot of the orchard, the stringy muscles of his forearms taut like drawn twine, then went to his toolshed for his garden harrow.

It was a fine old tool, held by many hands before his, the wooden haft stained dark with ages of sweat and dirt and dust. He sat to spare his knees, and looked out on a sky beginning to twinkle its first stars. He hadn't used the harrow in years, and the neglect showed in pits of rust and dull wood. His stomach growled with urgency, but there was still work to do and not much time left to do it. He satisfied himself with a drink of water, dribbled some on the haft then absently rubbed at the dirt to expose the rich grain beneath. It was beautiful wood, as hard as a thighbone and as lustrous as the finest furniture if only it were clean.

It seemed desperately important to him now that this instrument look its finest on this tragic day. He drizzled oil onto a rag and went to work on the haft, polishing in short strokes at first but then in longer swipes as the true beauty of the wood began to emerge. The wood gleamed now in the small light of his lantern, gleamed as he had never seen it, and then with a start he noticed an etching in the wood that had previously been concealed by dirt. He held the haft to the light, canted it this way and that until shadow set the etching in relief and he saw that a single letter, *H*, had been carved into the haft, and he sat back, lightheaded.

H for Hector, it must be, gone unnoticed for generations until now. Hector himself had held this harrow, the Hector of the long past whose duty to the future had brought the orchard into being and whose legacy would endure season after season so long as the orchard thrived.

Who would know Hector's name once Brussard was gone? No one, but what would it matter so long as the trees still grew to bear their fruit? Strangers could sit below the apple trees and marvel at the fragrance of the blossoms and the sweetness of the fruit never knowing who had cultivated it all, but Hector would be there just the same, and Brussard would be with him.

Where does duty finally lie, at the end or with the beginning? Brussard wrestled with this as the moon rose, casting the orchard in shimmering silver. He knew his days were short regardless. This did not frighten him, he had accepted the eventuality long ago, as had those in their turns before him. If the orchard lived then he lived, his sons lived, his fathers lived, they all lived in the sweetness of a blushing peach or ruby apple. Where was there room for hate in such a legacy?

He went into the house to do what he must, came back out leaving the doors unlocked and with a painful spasm in his stomach. Myriad points of light spangled the hills now, flowing inexorably downward. The moon was bright, casting shadows at night. Brussard sat against his apple tree of earlier and watched as the lights advanced, as the moon followed its course, as the dark deepened. The next spasm was wrenching. He doubled over, fought for breath, then forced himself back against the tree, forced his lips into a smile, forced himself to reach behind and stroke the tree lovingly as the poison at last sent him to his rest.

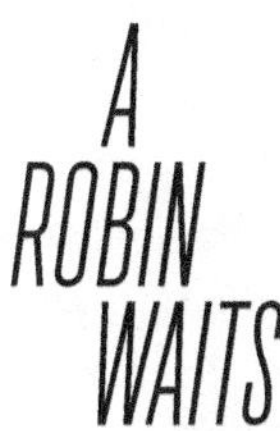

ROBIN LURAY KEPT A DIARY that would disturb anyone who happened to chance upon it.

I chanced upon it in the summer of '96 at a thrift store in Louisville, on a cluttered shelf where it had sat beneath a layer of dust for who knows how many years. My wife was fond of antique curios, so I had stopped in to see what might simultaneously catch my eye and please her as well. A thoughtful gift would be just the thing to ease the latest friction between us, which would soon become terminal regardless. No gift would have averted it.

I noticed the diary right away, as if it were ordained that it make its way to me after its long quiescence. It was about the size of a hardcover book, its pillowed boards crazed with age. It had tarnished nickel edging and, remarkably, a binding that remained as tight as when it had first been sewn. But what drew my attention was the alluring cover art, a vibrant scene of two Victorian women at picnic beside a pond. The colors, despite the dust and crazing, were resplendent with rich green grass and arresting blue water. Fish leapt in quicksilver arcs. Swans as white as angels poked and paddled through the rushes, while bees browsed energetically among a feast of luminous wildflowers. The sky was puffy and blue and perfect.

What really captured my imagination, though, were the two women, both with porcelain complexions and dressed in the layered frippery of the era, white lace and the cool linens of summertime, hats graceful and completely impractical shading eyes that met each other with something akin to mischief. The unknown artist had succeeded in recreating the beating hearts of those two women, and something more. The blush of a cheek, a lip pinched between teeth just so, a glimpse of a bare ankle, and a delicate, elegantly manicured hand reaching across, perhaps toward the picnic basket or perhaps to caress the sun-warmed ankle. There was nothing prurient about the portrait whatsoever, and yet it portrayed illicit love to my mind, and desire, and with these hope and longing.

I wondered if there would be a way to frame the covers, or at least somehow ascertain the artist. Neither would prove practicable, nor did I ever present the gift to my wife, because after blowing the dust away and thumbing the diary open my eyes fell upon this early entry, dated in May of 1936:

Black soot settled into cracks and crevices in weathered clapboard walls, tracing maps of peeling paint and buckling wood. Soot powdered windowsills, sifted through screens onto fine lace doilies. It caught the wind off of rusty tin roofs, streaming like fine black snow. We all wore it around our eyes and noses like ghoulish Halloween paint. We left handprints on the doorposts, little black fingers and palms on the lower part, bigger ones up high, like the gnarled, coal-skeined hands that found me in my nightmares, probing in the dark, as suffocating as the deepest mines

This was evocative if austere prose, appearing as it did between the more mundane musings of daily life, of milkmen in dandy white, and being awoken by hooves clomping down the street at night; of missives about the weather, and misgivings about schoolwork. During my thirty years as an English teacher, no student had ever impressed me with such elaborate imagery. I was intrigued—no, enthralled—so I kept the diary for myself, reading it during those estranged weeks as my marriage dissolved once and for all, taking note where the ink ran (from tears?), and where a page had been torn out (shame?). I puzzled through hastily scrawled passages, letters unleashed on the page by a hand that couldn't keep pace with a mind. It was at once thrilling and mysterious, but above all, it was viscerally disturbing.

The diary covers a span of six years. Robin Luray was only ten when she wrote the passage above. What an incredible mind she had, to have been able to arrange words with such dexterity and at such an early age. There is no likeness of her in the diary, and no other likeness that I have ever discovered. She never described herself, and yet I pictured her in my mind, tall for her times but not gangly, a thick mop of hair that was as black as the coal mines of her nightmares, a round face, petite nose, pensive lips, and a penetrating gaze that would unsettle the sternest of men. She wore overalls, never dresses—even on Sundays—but did not consider herself to be a tomboy, simply practical in her attire.

The town she describes is Burnham, Kentucky, one of those insular, east-Kentucky towns huddled in the hollows of densely forested hills that belie the trauma of the coal mines tunneling beneath them. The town is an outpost of mining with no redeeming features despite the natural beauty that bestrides it. It has no grand history, no memorable moments, and no outsider to mourn it if it were to be blown into the forest by a freak storm. In one musing Robin worries that someday the entire town might collapse into the catacombs below, like an anthill under a horse's hooves, neither remembered nor lamented. It must have been a dreary existence, dreary enough in present day Appalachia but especially so in depression-era times.

Her diary begins shortly after her father was killed in a cave-in. She described him as a large man, remarkably gentle, albeit with a hacking cough and rough hands that bore the perennial stain of coal dust. Her mother, Orella, was a buxom woman with a stern countenance who kept her graying hair in a bun, wore a red-checkered apron that hung to her tattered hem, kept chickens and tended a garden, and was continually fretting about one thing or another. Robin had an older brother, Leroy, whom she barely abided, and a younger brother, Lemuel, who had been a fussy baby but was now a timid presence who kept to the corners. A few aged photos on their mantel were of men wearing uniforms of gray and with faraway looks in their eyes, although exactly who these men were was never explained to her.

The loss of her father was devastating, both emotionally and materially. She noted that her mother never cried, but instead berated her father for leaving them in such desperate straits. Salvation came in the form of her father's brother, Uncle Tate, also a miner and providentially unmarried. Uncle Tate moved in to care for the family, although what began as a godsend soon revealed an uglier character.

Uncle Tate did not resemble his brother at all, except for his coal-skeined hands. Uncle Tate was thin, almost skeletally so, with a wiry gray beard that made him seem to be the older of the two brothers. He had a smell that Robin couldn't describe, she having not yet been exposed to alcohol sweats and unwashed sex. Despite these vulgarities, Robin felt safe with her uncle, felt safe sitting on his knee, his hand caressing her thigh. She would have called him her favorite uncle, as if he weren't the only uncle she had for comparison. Under his guiding authority, life in the Luray household eventually settled back into its dreary routine.

Robin resumed her more mundane musings, breakfasts each morning (always eggs and grits, sometimes a slice of bacon), scooping honey from the hollow of a tree and then licking it from her fingers, Leroy's incessant and increasingly brutal bullying of both her and Lemuel, a dramatic day when the sheriff shot a rabid dog. Her mother's not warm older sister Jewel, who worked in the church and had no children, stopped in to visit periodically. Some people called Aunt Jewel a spinster, which sounded lewd to Robin and so she was too embarrassed to ask anyone what it meant, including her priggish teacher, who kept the school's sole and well-worn dictionary carefully locked away.

Robin's life is colorless to be sure, although by no means uncommon, so from her perspective all is well. But then her entries begin to take on a darker tone, whole days, sometimes an entire week skipped like stutters in time. This is where the passage that first caught my attention appears, and from then on, when she does write, her entries know no sunlight. She writes of crushing weight, of stabbing pain and dank sheets. She awakens in the sultry mornings feeling battered by her nightmares, hugging herself and unable to discern reality from the images her mind stirs in the darker hours. Lemuel, who sleeps on a pallet across from her, keeps his back to her now. He is often awake, though. She can tell because he strokes his ear as he sucks his thumb.

As she approaches her eleventh birthday she is a spiritless rag doll of a girl with shadows under her eyes. Leroy's bullying suddenly takes a turn toward hateful words coupled with accusations that leave their own wounds. He is getting bigger, some whiskers sprouting on his chin of late. He won't meet her eyes. She sits quietly at the breakfast table and no one will meet her eyes except Uncle Tate, who smiles fondly and pats her on the head. She doesn't like being patted this way, as if she were a pet. She doesn't like his touch now. She wants him to leave, and she finally works up the courage to ask her mother to send him away.

She approaches her mother in the kitchen. Aunt Jewel is there, gossiping about this and that, but Aunt Jewel goes silent when Robin comes in. Aunt Jewel seems to notice something out the window and focuses her attention there. Orella is wringing her hands. The dialogue must have gone like this:

"Mama?" Robin says, desperately nervous. "I have nightmares."

Orella clucks with disconcern and waves it off. "All children do, baby."

Robin is tipping and peering to make eye contact with her mother, who works just as diligently to avoid it. She's still wringing her hands. With a gulp, Robin says, "Please send Uncle Tate away."

There would have been a gasp, a fleeting, worried glance from Aunt Jewel. "We can't do that, baby," Orella would have said with a trembling lip. "He's our family."

The air rushes out of Robin, who seems to sag by inches. She turns around and leaves, uttering not another word, but lingers beyond the door to hear what might be said in her absence.

"Poor girl," says Aunt Jewel.

"I don't know what to do," says Orella.

"There's nothing to do. You've also got two boys to think about. He treats 'em good, and he keeps food on the table. She'll forget all about it when she gets older."

Robin can't bear to listen any longer.

A week passes without a word in her diary, and then Robin writes this:

How do you know if something is bad? How can you tell when a nightmare is real? The darkness hurts, the birds don't sing in the morning, and the sun passes overhead without lighting the day. No one sees me, not my teacher, not the sheriff, not my own mother. People whisper when I walk by, as if every-

body knows something shameful about me that I don't. What would Daddy tell me to do? He would have a story (I smile), something simple but meaning- ful that I would have to think about for a long time before I would understand. But that's the way his lessons always worked, so that I would remember them, not like Mama, who's too worried to be worried about me, or my teacher, who thinks I imagine things for attention, or the sheriff, who couldn't be bothered. Daddy would tell me to watch the robins in the field, how they stand and wait before they pounce, while the other birds flit and fly and wear themselves out. That would be Daddy's lesson, that a robin waits.

Robin is beginning to bud womanhood from her youthful body as she passes twelve years old. She writes less of nightmares and more of these pressing matters, of shirts that no longer fit properly and of the sudden long looks of boys. She has no interest in boys and shrugs them off, although they behave as if she is withholding something that is fun- damentally theirs. They react angrily. They call her disgusting names. The worst offender is an older boy named Bobby Trane, who corners her after school one day and presses her against a tree. "C'mon, we know you like it," he says lewdly. She tries to push him away but she isn't strong enough. He shoves a hand into her overalls and grins. His teeth are yellow and ugly. She tells him to stop, but this only eggs him on. He pinches her cheeks together painfully before she can cry out. His fingers are too strong, too intractable. Struggling against him is futile and she knows it. She doesn't submit but she doesn't fight any longer either. There is nothing she can do but wait.

She takes to going out alone at night, walking under the owls and away from all the eyes she has come to abhor. It rained earlier, a deluge that still drips from the trees and runs silty in the gutters. No one else is out on a night like this. Tinny music blares from the bar up the street. The bar is a bad place, but she doesn't turn away. The men inside will never know she passed by. She plashes through the oily mud out front. A bare bulb above the front door provides the only light.

She is passing behind a flatbed truck that smells of creosote when the bar's screen door bangs open, drawing its spring in a taut, creaking thrum. The sheriff totters out onto the planked porch, staggers off the porch and into the mud, swaying woozily as he goes. He hacks a cough, then doubles over to wretch into the mud. Robin watches through the smeared windows of the flatbed. The sheriff straightens himself up unsteadily and then plods to his patrol car. He's drunk as a skunk, that's what her daddy would say, slobbering drunk, full to his eyeballs. The sheriff passes out and falls into a puddle, lies sputtering in three inches of water.

Robin walks to him then, squats hands on knees for a closer look. This is the same sheriff who so casually brushed her aside when she went to him last year, as if she possessed no mind worth mentioning, only a body that wasn't hers to keep. His face is in the water. With one handful of his pomaded hair she could easily tug his face out of the water, but instead she watches and waits, fascinated. Bubbles plink and pop, cling to his hair like the sticky eggs of frogs, then the bubbles slow, and then they stop. She squats there for the longest time before she woodenly lifts herself and walks deeper into the night.

The sheriff's death caused a stir in Burnham, excited gossip beneath a veneer of sorrow that such an exalted man should meet his end that way. The more generous insisted that he had died doing his duty, chasing a gangster perhaps, or some other miscreant. How dare anyone sully his memory? Who was there to see it, after all? Anything could have happened.

Yes, who was there to see it, to see death come for the likes of the sheriff? Robin's entries come self-assured now, no longer the musings of mundane life or the recitations of nightmares, but comments with a purpose.

I am me, she writes. *I am my own. I will wait.*

Uncle Tate's room was upstairs. When he would come down at night, through the still darkness of the old house, he would tiptoe on the creaking floorboards as if to conceal a progress that fooled no one. Little Lemuel played with marbles and jacks, and had a toy truck to roll them around in. Sleeping with thumb in mouth and with his back to her as always during these latter nights, Robin takes the toys and sets them at the top of the stairs, then withdraws to her darkened doorway and waits.

There was no appointed hour. Robin always wondered what stirred him when it did, but come he would regardless the hour. On that night he stirs in the small hours, the only sounds the moaning of an old house in a soughing wind, a ticking clock, and the nocturnal scratching of mice in the walls. Lemuel occasionally whimpers at some disturbing dream. Robin can hear her own heartbeat, then the swoosh of a well-oiled door, a padded step, and then another. Time seems to stretch. A floorboard creaks for agonizing minutes before the next foot falls. Robin holds her breath lest it be heard, and then a howl of pain pierces the night, an offensive intrusion between slumbering walls, followed by the thump, thump, thump of a tumbling body, and then stillness again as if the night were undeterred.

A rustling from her mother's room, the swish of covers and the click of a lamp. Quick now. Robin darts to the landing, can sense his heat in the darkness. She lowers an ear, detects halting breaths, and she nearly cries. It isn't done, it wasn't enough, and another wait would be cruel fate. She feels out with a foot, touches his scratchy neck with her bare toes, inhales sharply and jumps. The snap is sickening, and must surely have been as loud as the fall. She backs away as her mother's door hushes open, casting a shaft of yellow light across her uncle, whose dead tongue lolls as if lapping at the floor. Bile burns the back of Robin's throat, but it is done.

My belief in the veracity of Robin's tale began to take a turn after this episode, for how could a little girl from such deprived circumstances have acquired the aptitude to commit such an act? I was desperate to think of her as a gifted innocent, not as a dispassionate murderess. I fully recognized that my own failure to produce children had jaded my perception. I projected into Robin what I would have wanted from a daughter, a spirited and precocious girl who knew words and how to order them artistically. What a joy that would have been, what a continuous source of pride.

I had to step back from this, to reinstate disbelief and take a more skeptical view. Robin had already demonstrated an uncanny mastery with words, perhaps she possessed a dark imagination to match, an imagination in the vein of Edgar Allen Poe, for instance, or Joseph Conrad. Perhaps she wasn't the innocent child I had made of her. This became even more evident when, some months later, she ventured away from Burnham and into an early winter's forest.

All was gray and damp and cold. The twisted trees looked deformed and menacing. Through her words I could feel the chill in my bones, from both atmosphere and apprehension. One of the old abandoned mines had its entrance in an ugly patch of woods, which had previously been a mature forest before being clear-cut to the loam and scattered limestone of its once healthy forest floor. The woods had since grown back tangled and twisted, dense with briars and poison ivy, and woven through with cloying plants that were exotic to the region. The rocks were sharp, some covered in a sickly olive moss. Spotted mushrooms gave off a pungent odor, and a few vile black snakes hadn't yet succumbed to hibernation.

She describes the mine entrance as a maw of ingratitude, slimy and slick and left long ago to find its way back to nature. The adults of Burnham haven't visited this mine in a generation, but the teenagers of Burnham know it well. Whiskey bottles and tin beer cans lay discarded at random. Soot runs up a wall from a lifeless fire ring, the charred wood like crumbling bones. There is a mattress that reeks of mouse urine, and blankets too filthy to wrap around even the most desperate of frigid shoulders. The place stinks of every depredation and turpitude imagin-able. Robin keeps a palm over her nose as she explores.

Farther into the depths, away from the licentious entrance and where darkness begins to swallow the light, there is less evidence of mayhem. The stench recedes, the air becomes musty and cool and with the density of deeper time. Rusty lanterns hang from support timbers, once lighting the way, now as cold and inert as the dark stone around them. It is death-ly quiet, no breeze, not a stir of it. The flame of her candle holds straight and steady. Footprints in the dirt had been left by grandfathers or even their grandfathers. She finds what she needs, a softer patch of ground beyond a scattering of loose stones. A support timber had slipped, a heavy drip of tar frozen in time on its exposed end. She gives the timber a light rap and steps quickly back. Dust rattles down, occluding the air around her. She sneezes, and then smiles thinly.

Orella wrung her hands these days until her knuckles were raw and tender. Leroy had quit school and had gone to work in the mines to pro-vide a few dollars for the family. Lemuel was taller than ever, although no less demure. Aunt Jewel had come down with heart palpitations so didn't get out as much, and Robin, now fourteen, had developed the nascent aspects of a woman, most of which she found to be a nuisance.

Hers was a mouth to feed that made no money. Her scribblings, however masterful, were inscrutable to Orella and weren't worth a nickel, and there was no other work in Burnham for a young girl. The mending was done by the older ladies, the baking the same. Robin was too young to tend bar, too recalcitrant to clean at the church or school, and too fragile to butcher hogs. Orella knew, hinting discretely at first and then more directly, that Robin would need to be married soon, which was not uncommon for girls of her age in those times. Robin would normally have spat that back at her mother in disgust, but instead she raised an intrigued eyebrow.

Bobby Trane was as aware of the Luray family's predicament as anyone else in Burnham. At sixteen he had already taken his place in the mines, shamelessly flaunting the few dollars he earned there. He still gawked at Robin when he saw her, drool pooling in his lip and threatening to spill. His earlier adventure had been all urgency and hot breath. It hadn't revealed the true nature of her litheness, and he was eager to see more. A match between the two was being discussed. He let it be known that he was amenable to whatever arrangements might be made.

Robin went for a walk with him on a Sunday afternoon, resisting his insistence that they hold hands. She did whisper in his ear, though, and he did flash his yellow grin, and so some nights later they met surreptitiously in the ugly woods and made their way to the old mine.

Leroy is well acquainted with the mine, although he has never ventured as deep as Robin leads him now. He is satisfied, though, when they pass beyond the rank smell and come upon a clean pallet that Robin has arranged far away from any possible prying eyes. Candles flutter and cast flickering shadows, while Leroy heats up enough to overwhelm the musty cold air. He lies with her. She seems tense, but doesn't object as his hands probe forbidden places. The rank air of the entrance would have been more tolerable than his breath, but Robin somehow maintains the pretense of submission. Still, she averts her lips when he tries to kiss her, and urges him back when he goes for the buttons of her overalls.

"Wait," she whispers huskily, her expression ambiguous in the undulating light. She stands. "I'll be right back."

Leroy grins in anticipation as Robin slips beyond the edge of the light, but then frowns as a few grains of soil dust down onto his face. Robin is somewhere ahead in the darkness, where ominous grating sounds emanate. More soil streams down, enough to stir a primal terror and send him to his feet. "What are you doing?" he hollers, and when no reply comes, he bolts.

In the dim light ahead he can just make out the incomprehensible silhouette of what appears to be Robin tugging at a rope. "What are you doing?" he hollers again. Robin's silhouette tugs with more urgency.

With sweat popping out on his forehead, Bobby sprints forward, racing as if his very life hangs on his next step. He reaches Robin and takes her by the shoulders, turns her. She kicks him in the knee and keeps pulling at her rope. Bobby sees it now, in a horror that contorts his face with realization and rage. He looks up at the creaking support timber, the trickles of soil coming down. Anger roils. He will kill her for this.

He whips out his knife, a wicked thing that has seen its share of mayhem. He lunges, slicing deeply into her right forearm. She cries out as warm blood runs from her fingers. She kicks viciously, drives him back. Her right arm hangs useless, but she still holds the rope firmly in her left hand; and with one last, desperate tug, the ceiling comes down.

No one questioned why Robin had taken to wearing long-sleeved flannel shirts in the summertime. All attention was instead on Bobby Trane, missing now for a week. The sheriffs were dumbfounded, his parents insistent that the boy would not have run off. It was Bobby's teenaged friends who eventually solved the mystery, for only teenagers ever visited the old mine, and they were the ones who reported the cave-in. Teams of worried miners took to the rubble until Bobby's mangled body was uncovered. No one could fathom why he would have gone alone into the mine, but teenaged boys often did unfathomable things. The incident soon gave way to more pressing matters, though, for war was brewing in Europe.

Any illusions I had of Robin were lost after that summer's entries. Her writing skill was clearly growing, her diary demonstrating the natural evolution of talent as it matures, which would seem to render her tale as fact. And yet I simply could not place the depravity of Robin's actions into the mind of a girl once so sweet. This had to be fiction, probably not written by a girl at all, but rather by someone of true literary prowess, the diary left behind like a breadcrumb of eccentricity. It was still a work of inspiring literary competence, though, so I continued to read, taking the tale as fiction from then on, albeit with an emptiness in the hollow of my chest.

Robin wore a long scar on her right arm as war broke out. Burnham practically emptied as its men were sent off to fight. Mines were closed or scaled back, and money became tighter than ever.

Aunt Jewel died alone in her bed, and had to be buried by the state for want of the funds to do it properly. Orella aged ten years in a day, and constantly harangued her fifteen-year-old daughter to find work. The family lived on eggs and the vegetables from their Victory Garden. Meat was scarce, and Lemuel was losing weight. Sometimes he would shyly bring home a squirrel to supplement their dinner. With hours scaled back at the mine, Leroy's contribution had scaled back as well.

Leroy was terrified of being drafted, a terror that infused Orella equally. Robin was also aware of her older brother's predicament. His cruelty might have left its mark, but his terror didn't touch her. Her thoughts ran off to words and the long walks she took alone. With fewer men around, she could walk during the day without the catcalls and pestering. For Robin it was a perfect time. She would sometimes sit alone in her room and gaze at her puckered scar, as if it were a map or an arrow pointing her toward an unknown fate. She kept her cuffs buttoned tightly. No one knew she bore the scar. Someday someone would find out and she would have to concoct an explanation, but for now it was hers alone, to bear, to study, to wield if necessary.

Leroy applied for a deferment from the draft. As the sole breadwinner for his family his case was sound. He waited anxiously for an answer as war raged around the world, as men began to return to Burnham missing parts of their bodies. He would awaken at night amid sweat-soaked sheets, bend over to be sick when a milkman with only one arm came to the step. Terror infused his every moment.

After an interlude of sweeter descriptions of her daily life coupled with vibrant observations of nature recovering from the intrusion of coal, I found that I had suspended disbelief once more despite my best efforts to maintain objectivity. At sixteen, Robin would have been flush with the beauty of youth. I can't imagine her as gaunt and hollow-eyed from hunger, and she wrote nothing to that effect. Such was the quality of her craft that I reimagined her as the brilliant innocent she had been at ten. Yes, war had left its wounds, and yes, hunger was a constant, but woven through this was the sudden, startling clarity of the air, the freshness of flowers unsoiled by coal dust, and the black-streaked houses slowly cleansed with each rain. The darkened aura of her prose persisted, although tempered by these brighter observations. No nightmares haunted her. The desperate circumstances of her family did not deter her.

Burnham did not receive mail daily, but rather twice a week, in what were two eventful days for young Lemuel. It was always he who raced to the mailbox, or sometimes even waited for the mailman to arrive, delivering Sears catalogs or other colorful publications. At a time before television, when the radio jarred with only the bleakest news, and when the nearest movie house was miles and miles away, these were his only distractions, the only way he could feed his imagination.

One day, as he raced to the mailbox, Lemuel pulled up short when he found Robin already there sifting the mail. He would certainly have felt betrayed by this, but as he was only ten, still innately insecure, and as his sister was now an adult from his perspective, he kept his dismay to himself. There would have been a conversation. Robin does not document their words, only the setting, but I'm sure that Lemuel, despite his shyness, would have said, in a pained and tenuous voice, something to the effect of, "I always do that."

From here I conjured my own scene, troubling though it was.

It is as if Robin doesn't notice him at all. She flips through the mail absently but then pauses at an official looking envelope. "What is it?" Lemuel asks.

"Shut up," is her uncharacteristically harsh response. She tears open the envelope, takes out the letter and studies it.

"Mama says you're not supposed to read other people's mail," Lemuel whines.

"I said, shut up," she shoots back. She holds up the letter and a devious smile crosses her lips. "Well, well, well," she muses, "it looks like Leroy got his deferment. Too bad."

"Huh?"

She folds the letter and pushes it into her overalls, takes Lemuel's shoulder and squeezes it hard.

"Don't you say anything," she says menacingly." Understand?"

Lemuel's blood seems to run cold. He nods nervously.

"Good," she says. "Now go somewhere and play. Go on!"

She pats his butt then, not hard, and he takes off, looking over his shoulder as he runs, and sees his sister marching up the steps, looking triumphant.

Unaware of his deferment, and with no document to release him from conscription, Leroy was drafted shortly thereafter; and before the leaves began to fall that autumn, he was killed in action somewhere in the South Pacific.

Orella sits in her rocker, wringing her hands and looking more like a grandmother now, while Lemuel seems to withdraw into himself, and Robin writes her final entry:

The old house is empty now, but not empty of its creaks and squeaks and moaning walls. Outside the sky is gray with rain, while inside it is gray with grief. Nature always takes its turn, revealing its seasons, while last year's leaves still litter the steps. Has the robin waited long enough? Is it now time for it to fly far from the lingering dust? What will await it when it waits no more?

There is a smear on that last line where a fat drop fell and was then rubbed with a knuckle. The next page has been torn out. What would have been the conclusion, then? How does the author reconcile such a story? I conjure my own ending. Spring arrives at last, a fresh, bright day that shouts with joy. Robin walks out, leaving Orella behind to reckon with her own guilt. In my imagining, Robin has Lemuel by the hand. The two start out down the road, reveling in the greenery and clean air, a walk long and arduous until they find a better place.

As the days and weeks passed, I could not put Robin's tale out of my mind. She would be seventy now, nearing the millennium and occupying a world so far removed from those years of her diary that it all must have receded to mere dream. I looked for her while my wife waged war on our marriage, convincing myself that my quest was nothing but simple distraction; but the more I looked, the greater became my doubts that Robin had ever been more than fiction. I searched phone books from Louisville to Lexington, made calls and dabbled at the World Wide Web, but found no reference whatsoever to a Robin Luray. This further compounded my doubts because an author of her skill could not have gone through the decades unnoticed.

At last, on a lark, I go to Burnham, a torturous drive on winding and barely maintained roads. There are no helpful records at the county seat, many having been lost in a fire in the fifties. Burnham itself is a derelict huddle of collapsing houses being reclaimed by a forest that has improved in character over the decades. Songbirds sound in treetops risen from former living rooms, while rusty equipment protrudes from draperies of kudzu, like the last remnants of a lost civilization. The main street is barely passable, and I am eventually forced to continue on foot.

It is eerie walking among these former homes, as if they watch me from their peeling paint and buckling wood, their rusty metal roofs loose and crashing a cadence in the wind. It is not death I feel here, but desolation, the utter, complete abandonment of lives once lived, however bleakly. One house still displays white paint under a sagging awning that has held the weather at bay. I climb crumbling cement steps and crunch across a forest floor of a yard to a front door that has come loose at its upper hinge. On the doorpost I see them, still clearly discernable after all this time, the sooty handprints of the former inhabitants, little black fingers and palms on the lower part, bigger ones up high.

iSIGHT

The lecture hall placed him on a postage-stamp of a stage below rising tiers of seats mostly empty save for the few students who deigned to attend. The hall could have sat hundreds, but he lectured to only a fraction of that, positioned as sparingly as chess pieces in the endgame, from low to high and none apparently paying attention.

With a sense of dismal irrelevance, he scanned his scattering of students. None looked askance at his pause; none leaned over to whisper a sarcastic comment in their neighbor's ear. Their eyes were on their phones, seemingly transfixed, fingers flitting through swipes while their cameras captured his lecture on video to laze over later. He often questioned why he still taught when he could have retired a decade ago. But in truth he knew the reason: he still yearned for the thrill of even that one eye-locking glimpse of inspired insight, the quickening of mind that would validate his efforts, although he hadn't made that level of eye contact in a long time.

One of his students, seated toward the middle and a few tiers up from the stage, was Ainsley Beck Cohen-Dyer, a comely junior whose appled cheeks, strong jawline and fair complexion lent her a classic beauty that was completely squandered in this era of digital distraction.

Her attention was also fixed firmly on her phone, eyes darting left and right in frenetic motion. Ainsley was given her pretentious and not-so-clever name by aging parents whose formative times predated the parents of all Ainsley's friends, bequeathing her an antique legacy that still dragged at her ankles. Her bespoke arrival was the singular, nauseatingly self-congratulatory event to grace her parents' lives, and so they had lavished upon her all the tedium they could conjure, beginning with her name, never once hesitating in their effusion to consider how easy it was for vicious little kids to corrupt *Ainsley* into *Anus*, or mock her initials, ABCD, in hurtful and ever-evolving ways. Ainsley went by Beck thereafter (which could have been short for Becky or Rebecca but wasn't), while her parents stubbornly clung to her given name in an eye-rolling display of wounded feelings and disappreciation.

Neither the professor nor the subject of the class made it even as far as her peripheral awareness. What had her full attention was an ad for the new iSight eyeglasses, now available with a click, delivered by drone, and potentially in her hands by the time her class wrapped up. She swiped through configurations and colors, modeled them on her face in real time using the embedded app, tipping this way and that to gauge how the earpieces would look against her fine, sandy hair—currently gathered in a short brushy ponytail—and how the frames might enhance her delicate eyelashes and add definition to a perky nose that she was convinced made her look like a teenager.

A text box intruded onto her screen. *U gonna get m*, the text asked. The text was from Landon. He already had a pair, betas obtained by some means that he never quite got around to explaining, although he harped on them constantly. The beta version was rather plain, actually, black-framed, bulky, but Landon wore them proudly; and from the day he first showed up with them on he seemed to look at her in a new way, with a sort of gawping reverence. She had been intrigued ever since

May b, she thumbed back.

They met after class in the murky air of the quad, amid listless grass and the permeating odor of burning wood. Somewhere there was a fire. There was always a fire—the news feeds displayed countless scenes—but the constancy of the blazes remained abstract, never coming closer than the gouts of orange mayhem they viewed on their screens. Ainsley could see her reflection in the dark lenses of Landon's glasses, a pair of unflattering portraits drained of color, and yet his expression, if that blank countenance could be called one, seemed fixated on her.

"What do you see?" she asked him self-consciously, clutching phone and tablet to her chest as if they were a barricade of books.

"I see you," he replied flatly.

"Well, stop it. You're creeping me out."

"Sorry."

They sat in silence, Ainsley folding her knees as if she were wearing a dress. Landon sat cross-legged, his hands back and flat on the grass, his vision roving through their surroundings and his lips parted in a sense of wonder. Landon wasn't particularly good-looking. He had unmanageable dark hair, pimples that simply refused to move on, and a smudge of whiskers below a too-thin nose, but all one noticed when looking at him now were his glasses, black and bulky but undeniably fascinating.

Ainsley thumbed at her phone, and then with a frown looked up to find Landon gazing off as distantly as if he were peering through binoculars. "How do you text with those?" she asked.

"Eye movements," he answered distractedly, craning to follow a sole bird backlit against the sky. "The instructions tell you how."

"Well I just texted you."

"I know."

She huffed at that. "Well I wish you could be more helpful, then. It's a lot of money, but all you can do is look around and be weird."

"It's different for everybody, Beck." Now he was looking across the way at another student who was wearing the glasses. They exchanged what could only be described as an inside look, although nothing in their expression revealed that. "You see what you're supposed to see, the way things really are."

"And how are things, really?"

"I told you—"

"Yeah, I know," she mouthed with pique. "It's different for everybody."

"Yeah, and you're missing out. You have no idea."

"Then let me try yours on."

"Naw," he shook his head, but he was still looking off at something she couldn't see. "You upload your phone into them, Beck. They're personalized. Mine wouldn't work on you, or...or I guess they would work but it would be weird."

"You can't tell me people don't share them sometimes."

"Maybe they do. I guess it could be kinda cool if you really knew somebody, but, yeah, I mean, do you let people go through your phone?"

She pulled back.

"*No*, that would be weird."

"Same thing."

His argument made sense, but did nothing to mollify Ainsley's sense of being purposefully excluded from an elite membership. Landon suddenly sat up straighter, the direction of his attention unreadable. "Hey, check it," he said. "Somebody saw a cougar up at the lake."

"A cougar?"

"Yeah."

"I thought they were extinct, or only in Mexico or something."

"They must be coming back. Isn't it cool?" Landon followed animal videos obsessively, so the rare sighting of an even rarer animal was something that would tend to get him worked up.

"I guess," she said without enthusiasm. She couldn't help but glance over her shoulder at what he might be seeing in the distance, even as she understood that he wasn't looking off anywhere, just reading a feed behind his lenses. With a quick flick at her phone, she stood and brushed dried grass from her jeans. "I gotta go."

"See ya."

Ainsley was walking into her dorm room when she got a text from her friend Kayla.

"*I got m*," the text read.

Ainsley thumbed a quick reply. "*Well?*"

"*Awesome!*" followed by a week's worth of emojis.

"*So tell me!!!*"

"*U gotta c 4 yrself.*"

"*Ugh!*" Ainsley thumbed in frustration.

She fell onto her bed, her phone held up but she found herself studying the ceiling instead, picking out patterns in the shadows and cracks in the uneven white paint. Her thumb moved as if disembodied and of its own accord. She made out a face in the shadow and texture of the ceiling, focused on it until it resolved into a woman's face in profile, a delicate jaw, cunning expression, and a wave of hair. Eyes blurring, she searched some more, found the beak of an eagle, or perhaps a falcon, the nostrils slightly off center but the pattern was plain. Crossing her eyes slightly, the nostrils became eyes and the beak became an aardvark, and then a cartoon character with a long nose. She tapped her thumb and it was done.

Her glasses arrived an hour later, delivered to her door by an unmemorable guy who spoke no words, just held out a faux machined-metal box with the letters *iSight* prismed in black on the top. The box sat comfortably and lightly in her hand. Their phones made the necessary communication and validation. As he turned away, the guy hesitated and looked back. "Cool," he said, both envious and awed.

She closed the door absently, her eyes on the box, so preternaturally light considering the magnitude of its contents, and felt a tingle in her fingers, a rising tremor that coursed up her spine and into the back of her brain, flowing down to tickle her breastbone until she couldn't endure the anticipation any longer. She lifted the lid with reverence and trepidation, set it carefully aside as if it might, too, hold some magic. She took out the glasses, sealed in a thin bubble wrap envelope. The package felt intricately fragile between her fingers, reminding her of the bones of a little bird. There were no instructions in the box. She carefully set it aside as well.

She cautiously snipped the end of the envelope with scissors, as if performing surgery, noting every detail. And then, after a deep breath, she reached in with nervous fingers, pulled the envelope away, and held her new glasses in the light.

She had chosen studious titanium frames, with oval lenses to soften her cheeks. The lenses were as dark as Landon's, which was disconcerting because they seemed the kinds of lenses a blind person would wear. A tag affixed to an earpiece read simply: Put Me On.

She slid the glasses into place, feeling the cool metal glide comfortably across her temples. She squeezed her eyes in anticipation, and with a last push with a middle finger, she seated the glasses on her nose. And then, with a squint at first, she opened her eyes to darkness.

"Wait...what?" she mumbled unsurely.

The earpieces vibrated almost imperceptibly, becoming warm, or was that her imagination? She was resisting the impulse to snatch the glasses off when a voice intruded, filling her mind from ear to ear with the resonance of someone speaking directly to her from outside the glasses, because that's how she now perceived anything beyond those dark lenses—outside, while she was inside—and the voice spoke to her: "Blink twice if you're ready to begin set-up."

It was a woman's voice, indeterminate, neither young nor old, soothing and secure. Ainsley blinked twice.

An image resolved before her eyes, bright sun and blue sky and startlingly green grass. A woman approached wearing a dress that flowed white in a soughing breeze, a breeze that Ainsley swore she could feel tickling softly in her ears. The woman's hair was golden and long, as free as a mare's mane, her face tranquil and ageless. The woman stopped at a discreet distance, folded her hands at her waist, and smiled beatifically. "I am 29Zebra16234T2Alpha6, your guide and tutor. That's a ponderous name, but don't worry. You'll be able to personalize it soon." Her voice was so gently harmonious that Ainsley thought the woman's long alphanumeric designation sounded like poetry. "We can now proceed with the gestures that will enable you to operate your new iSight glasses. Blink twice when you're ready."

Ainsley went to lie down, feeling her way to her bed. She knew from Landon and Kayla, as well as her own research, that the set-up process could be time consuming and deeply personal. She should really be reviewing the lecture from this morning, but her excitement won out. She could always review the lecture later, why else make a video of it? And her roommate Aleks had labs today, which meant that Ainsley would have complete privacy for most of the afternoon.

She settled on her pillow, hands on her stomach, while 29Zebra (because that is what Ainsley imprinted as an appropriate and somewhat exotic name for her tutor) waited with timeless patience. Ainsley snugged her shoulders, took a breath, and blinked twice.

29Zebra smiled in gratitude, then dispersed pixel by pixel into the screensaver, which was a live-motion nature scene complete with the sounds of swishing grass, the rustle of water, and the whistling of wind in the rocks of a high ridge. It was nature as perfection, peaceful and calm. Ainsley's eyes grew heavy, snatched back from sleep when 29Zebra reappeared, speaking in a voice no less pleasant but definitely more authoritative. The tutorial proceeded.

One blink, two blinks, left blink, right blink...there was surgical intervention that would allow advanced users to view both lenses independently. Ainsley swallowed queasily and blinked no. 29Zebra smiled maternally. "Of course," she said. "That's a big step. We will proceed stereoscopically."

The basic operation was easy, that is, using the glasses as if they were a phone she could wear on her face, using eye blinks for taps. Texting and emailing, though, took skill and memory. 29Zebra coached her through it. It was almost exhausting.

Eventually, Ainsley had command of these functions, as well as personalized menus, and was now ready for the biggest step yet. 29Zebra spoke:

"Good work, Beck. If you would now provide permission so that I may upload your phone."

Ainsley felt queasy again, but she clenched her teeth, blinked her assent, and gripped her sheets as if she might fall.

Photos, music, texts, social media posts...the algorithms gathered it all, the minutiae as well as the major moments; her videos, e-books, and calendar; her likes and dislikes—her very essence. It took time.

Ainsley settled in once more, no longer drowsy. She noticed with a start that the nature scenes were becoming transparent, and that within them she could begin to make out vague images of her room, which continued to materialize until they were clear and sharp although limned with the tangerine shades of a particularly vivid sunset. She raised eyes to the ceiling and searched for the pattern of the face she'd found earlier. She found it and more.

Ainsley gawked. The face seemed to descend from the ceiling amid an ethereal swirling of color, like a Hubble image of a distant nebula, and this color flowed outward to encompass her entire vision, except for the face in profile, which gained details and features in a steady evolution that rendered it in three dimensions, and so lifelike that Ainsley found herself reaching up to touch the celestial skin of its cheek, so sure from her senses that the face was there and solid that she gave a little lurch to close the distance and was confused when her fingers touched only air.

She drew back and allowed her vision to wander over the swirling ether, dove back in with force of will and this time she found the eagle—and it *was* an eagle, not a falcon—and not just a beak, but now with wings and a bright white head and the fierce golden gaze she knew from photos; and then the swirling palette absorbed the eagle, her vision cleared, returning to her sunset-limned room, and 29Zebra announced that the upload was complete.

Ainsley felt refreshed, although she also felt certain that her eyes should have been strained to exhaustion after all of that. Her once-austere dorm room was now opulent. It seemed larger, much larger. Her cheap desk appeared to be made of the richest lacquered wood. Aleks' bed looked like a canopied cushion of cloud, now apparently far enough away that Ainsley would no longer be able to sling her legs over and prop her feet on it. When Aleks suddenly burst into the room, Ainsley gawked once more.

"Whoa," Aleks said, pulling back into the doorway in surprise. "So you actually did it. You pulled the trigger."

Ainsley heard the words, and would have commented immediately if she weren't so overawed by what she saw. Aleks, always athletically pretty, fairly shimmered with an aura of vitality, a smile brighter than polished ivory blazing from her ebony face. She was so overwhelmingly beautiful that Ainsley felt a churning need to reach out and run the back of her hand along that flawless skin.

Aleks frowned. "Now you're acting weird like Landon," she said.

"Oh, sorry." Ainsley slid the glasses off and was immediately plunged into the depressing reality of their dorm room. Aleks was staring at her oddly.

"So what's it like?" Aleks asked. She pushed the door closed and flopped onto her bed, once again close enough for Ainsley to rest her feet. Aleks slung her own legs over onto Ainsley's bed, and the two lay like a bridge over the gap. Ainsley cupped the glasses protectively on her stomach.

"It's wild," she said. "Everything's so enhanced."

"Enhanced enough to be worth all that money?" Aleks asked skeptically.

"Yeah, I think so."

"Well I sure hope so." Aleks wasn't a fan of the glasses. She knew a few people who had bought them, and didn't like the way those people now mooned and fawned and gazed at everything as if they were in a fairytale. Still, the phone aspects were practical. If they could turn off all the other stuff and make the price reasonable, she might consider buying a pair for herself. And the frames did compliment Beck's features, it was only that the dark lenses were so disturbing. "Isn't it weird, though?" Aleks went on. "I mean, all I can see are black lenses, but you see everything in—what?—Wizard of Oz colors or something?"

"It's more than that." Ainsley slipped the glasses back on, got up on her elbows, and Aleks again became an Olympian. "But I only just finished uploading them. They're supposed to adapt as you go. Hmm. I wonder what it's like to look in a mirror?"

She hopped up and went to their worn and drooping dresser, which now appeared elegant enough to reside in the Louvre. Ainsley saw herself perfectly proportioned, including her formerly nondescript nose, which now provided just the right amount of mature definition, lending her face a studiously academic look while remaining charmingly attractive at the same time. Oddly, her reflection was not wearing glasses.

"Ohmygod, I look amazing!" Ainsley gushed in awe.

"You're pretty already, Beck. You don't need glasses for that."

That comment went unheard. Ainsley wondered how she would look with blue eyes, blinked through the menus until she found it, then made the selection. "Oh, man," she gasped.

"What?" asked Aleks.

"Blue eyes are the best." Her eyes were normally a warm brown, so the icy cool of blue gave her a startling appearance.

"Really, Beck? Really?" Aleks said with an incredulous lift of brows. "You can get contacts for that, you know."

Ainsley blinked and her eyes became green. No, she liked blue better. "This works too," was all she said.

"But what does it matter if nobody can see?"

Ainsley frowned. "Yeah, you're right. But still...you should see your-self in these. You look like a goddess or something."

"I look like that all the time," Aleks grinned back immodestly.

"You wanna try 'em on?" Ainsley asked.

Aleks took an eager breath to answer yes, but then closed her mouth and pursed her lips. "No, I don't think so," she said hesitantly. "It's too personal, isn't it? That's what Landon always says."

"Landon can be a dick sometimes."

"And sometimes he's right." Aleks hopped up from the bed. "I gotta go before it gets too late."

Ainsley looked out their window into a world of wonder, every color richer, almost wet in its intensity, the murk gone, the sky an indescribable blue, the sun a low orb of golden oil shimmering above the rooftops across the way. "Wow, it's late, isn't it." Ainsley mouthed. "I've been do-ing this all day and it doesn't even feel like it. Where do you have to go?"

"Some of us are going to the lake to hang out, and maybe see a cou-gar somebody spotted."

"Really? Landon was saying something about that."

"Yeah, who knows, maybe we'll get lucky, but we need to get there before dark. You should come. Landon's going."

"He is? He didn't say anything."

"Sounds like Landon. We're gonna make a campfire, do hot dogs and marshmallows—you know, the whole outdoorsy thing."

"That sounds like it could be cool," Ainsley said noncommittally. She wasn't that enthusiastic about hanging out by the lake after dark, but she couldn't pass up the chance to show off her new glasses, especially if Landon was going to be there. And then she was intrigued by what the lake and the forest would look like through her new glasses, not to mention a campfire, or a canopy of stars far from the light pollution of campus. "Sure, yeah," she said after those thoughts mulled. "That sounds great."

Aleks drove, her earbuds in and her phone propped up in its holder. Ainsley gazed out the window in wonder. The people she saw were all bronzed and toned and as beautiful as a Greek myth. The cars going by looked new enough to have been driven out of showrooms that morning, while the houses and buildings along the way resembled nothing less than luxury on display—and around all of it, the people, the cars, the buildings and the trees, was an aura of light, the intense pinks and lavenders and oranges of the sunsets ever since those far-off fires had flared up.

Ainsley blinked a text to Aleks, and Aleks grinned over blindingly as her old car sputtered toward the lake, a sputter that sounded dismayingly odd against the unrivaled elegance Ainsley made of the car through her glasses. Aleks streamed a song, and Ainsley blinked in to stream the next. Both grinned at that. Ainsley was starting to get the hang of it now.

They reached the lake while the sun was still high enough to glitter golden on the placid water. Tendrils of smoke lifted from beyond a far ridge, as if from a line of winter chimneys, but to Ainsley they looked like gossamer threads of sea mist above an emerald coast. Aleks rubbed her eyes and scrunched her nose. Ainsley smelled the smoke too, but her visual senses seemed to keep the odor tamped down to insignificance in the background.

They got out and locked the car. "So where is everybody?" Ainsley asked.

"See over there?" Aleks pointed to a rocky outcrop well around the curve of the lake. "On the other side of that rock. That's where we're supposed to meet."

"That's a long way," Ainsley said with a hint of dread.

"It's not that far. C'mon."

They set out along the lake, which to Ainsley could have been an enormous pool of mercury lapping at the shore. Fish, breaching too quickly for Aleks to see, were reinterpreted for Ainsley to appear as diamond figurines arcing in silver tracery above the surface. The trail turned into the woods, which resembled a well-manicured arboretum rather than the tangled and desiccated woods they actually were. Ainsley tripped on a rock, which took on the countenance of a smiling turtle. She swore as she regained her balance, wagging a scolding finger at the turtle, which drew an eye roll from Aleks.

"Almost there," Aleks said.

They came back out along the lake, the sun now flattening against the ridge like a drop of liquid amber. Ainsley blinked for the elapsed time and sighed. Twenty-eight minutes of walking and stumbling, but they were almost there.

The sun dripped a last drop of golden luminance on the far ridge, and then dark engulfed them all at once. Aleks tapped on her phone light. "Do you need to take those off?" she asked.

"No," Ainsley said, amazed. "I can see fine. It's like infrared or something," although the shadows still appeared deep and menacing even if outlined in color. The woods were the same dark presence, heavy and brooding over their shoulders, glowing on the periphery where the first starlight penetrated, and shot through here and there with streaks of light, like fireflies in fast-forward.

They rounded the rock into an even deeper darkness. Aleks shone her phone around in confusion while to Ainsley everything appeared to be limned as usual, in a glow that revealed only presence, not detail. Aleks' eyes were discs of silver in a dark setting without contour, ghost like, worried perhaps, and now Ainsley was worried, too; and then something dense, dark, and lumbering jumped out of the shadows and screamed, "*Surprise!*"

Both Ainsley and Aleks jumped to catch their hearts before the organs could leap out into the woods. Laughter surrounded them. A big flashlight clicked on, dimmed and interpreted instantly by Ainsley's glasses. Landon's grin was so wide that Ainsley struggled not to slap it.

"Dammit, Landon. What the f—?"

"Hey, we're just having fun."

"Landon, you dick," Aleks simmered, patting her chest.

The others came out of hiding, Colby, Kayla, and a guy named Kean whom Ainsley didn't know. Introductions were made. What struck Ainsley at once was that neither Landon nor Kayla appeared to be wearing their glasses, although Ainsley intuitively knew, perhaps by the richer aura around their heads, that both had them on. And then, as her heart slowed, she noticed how totally gorgeous Landon was, how his hair fell just right, how smooth his skin and how perfectly proportioned his nose.

"So whaddaya see?" he asked Ainsley.

Still fuming, she bit back, "I could ask you the same."

"And now that you understand, I can tell you. I see the finest looking girl in the world."

Ainsley blushed away her indignation and gave him a coy smile. "You're not so bad either."

"Okay you two, get a room," Aleks said in a huff. "You guys scared the crap out of me."

"All in fun," Colby said in his dry, practical way. "Now it's dark and I can't see a damn thing, so let's get the fire going."

Colby was a big lumberjack of a guy, ostensibly with Kayla but relationships were always fluid. Kayla looked great with or without the glasses, although her iSight rendering made her resemble a super hero, or super assassin, what with the hard body, black hair, and bold bust. Kean was a reserved, wiry guy who spoke in a Scottish brogue. Ainsley pictured him in tartan, and expected him to raise bagpipes at any moment.

They found a clear spot farther around the outcrop, with a sliver of silver lake in view, a great swath of bejeweled, inkily fluid sky, and the darkly oppressive woods at their backs. There were rocks and logs for seating, and an acrid-smelling fire ring. While the others settled in, Kayla rummaged through her backpack for hot dogs and marshmallows. Colby gathered pine needles and twigs into a large heap in the fire ring, thumbed his lighter, and the entire heap flared up and burned itself out before Kayla could even get the hot dogs opened. Ainsley instinctively jerked back from the flare, which engulfed the entirety of her vision like a blast, if only for an instant. Landon caught her and chuckled. The two were sitting together on a log, with Aleks seated on a rock nearby and Kayla across the fire ring from them. Kean was leaning against the outcrop, gazing intently at the lake.

"You'll get used to that," Landon said. "Pretty soon your glasses will adapt and that won't happen anymore."

"Man, it was so fast. I feel like I should be blind or something."

"Don't worry, the glasses won't let that happen."

"You'll need to get bigger sticks," Kayla told Colby with a biting smile.

"Ya think?" Colby said flatly. "I'll be back." He crunched off into the woods.

Kean sidled over, his arms crossed tightly. "You can see the glow of the fire on the other side of the ridge. Do you think it's safe to make a campfire here?"

That was directed at no one, but Kayla spoke up. "We're by the lake and we've got a fire ring. I think it's okay."

"And I'm starving," Aleks said. "So it has to be okay." Kean shrugged and returned to his place by the outcrop. Aleks leaned in closer to Landon. "Have you—you know—hooked up with them on?" she asked in a conspiratorial whisper.

"Not yet," Landon grinned. He bumped shoulders with Ainsley. "So you wanna try it?"

Ainsley bit her tongue. "Hmm..." she mused with a sly smile. Through his glasses, Landon saw her eyes sparkle flirtatiously.

"I doubt we'll be seeing the cougar now," Kean commented from his place by the rock. "Too dark. And I was rather looking forward to it. Much like a lynx, I would think."

"Bigger than that, Kean," Kayla said.

"A pair of lynxes, then. We still have a few in the Highlands. Beautiful creatures."

Just then there was a crash in the woods.

"What was that?" Ainsley asked, halfway to her feet and twisting to look back at the impenetrable forest.

"Probably just Colby screwing around," Landon and Kayla answered simultaneously. They listened for more sound, but heard nothing but the rush of the breeze in the treetops.

"I'll go have a look," Kean said before loping into the woods. They all followed his footfalls in silence until they could hear them no more.

"I'm not going to let Colby get me again," Aleks said firmly. She walked over to Kean's place by the outcrop. "Beck," she hollered, "you should come see this."

The lake surface was so calm that the sky seemed to lap at their feet, the Milky Way a torrent of spectral light. Ainsley gasped at the enhanced image, which seemed to coalesce all around her in stardust and infinity, as if she could reach out and scoop stars into her palms like glittering grains. She raised her hands high, face bathed in the sky, eyes now closed and fingers spread wide as if to embrace creation.

"It's awesome, yeah?" Aleks breathed.

"You—have—no—idea," Ainsley breathed back.

They returned to the fire ring after that transfixing moment, the glossy sheens on their cheeks evaporating as they left the softness of the starlight for the mocking white of Kayla's flashlight. Kayla was bent over, rummaging again through her backpack, the flashlight shining upward and casting ghoulish shadows along the sides of her face. "Damn, I forgot to bring cokes," she grumbled.

Ainsley looked through the funnel of light to her place across the fire ring. "Where's Landon?" she asked with a start.

Kayla jerked her chin up. "He was just there." She stood and searched around in the limpid light. "Those guys," she muttered, hands on hips. "They're up to something. C'mon guys!" she hollered into the woods. "Cut it out!"

The three trained their ears but could hear nothing in the woods beyond the breeze and the eerie clicking of limbs. Kayla reared back with a bellow. "*C'mon guys!*" She stomped to the edge of the woods in disgust, hands now fisted on her hips, and peered into the depthless darkness. "The glasses don't help," she said. "I can't see a thing."

"I wonder what—" Ainsley began, but in the instant before she could finish, Kayla seemed to double backward from her belly and was violently yanked into the dark of the woods.

Ainsley and Aleks screamed and stamped in place, clutching each other in shock and fright. There was a deep crashing in the woods that ceased abruptly, and sounded close enough to probe with an outstretched foot if they dared.

"Something's out there," Ainsley whimpered.

"We gotta get out of here," Aleks exhaled all at once, her feet already in motion.

The two bolted around the outcrop and then onto the trail along the lake, all but blind in their panic. Athletic Aleks was the stronger runner. She got out ahead quickly, driven by nothing but primal fear, a fear that overrode her senses and sensibilities. Ainsley stumbled to keep up, but finally tripped where the trail turned back into the woods; and when she looked up from scuffed hands and knees, Aleks was gone.

"Aleks!" she screamed. "*Aleks!*"

Alone in the light-limned dark, face slick with tears, and urgently slipping and clawing to get to her feet, she made a shuddering and hapless query. "29Zebra, where's Aleks?"

"Your friend has disappeared into the forest."

That ageless voice, once so soothing, now sounded blithely insouciant.

"What do you mean, *disappeared?*" Ainsley cried in frustration. She was unsteadily on her feet now, the dark woods clamping down like a constricting snake. The starlight over her shoulder etched malevolent tracers on her retinas.

"I can enhance the darkness,"—that same, agonizingly neutral tone—"but I can't resolve it. Your friend went beyond my ability to discern shape from shadow."

"Ohmygod! Did something get her?"

"That's impossible to know. I can replay a recording of the moment if you wish."

If she could have reached through her glasses to strangle 29Zebra, she would have done it. "No..." she uttered, feeling the clammy darkness against her skin. Her tears were making her lenses fog, scattering the night impenetrably across her vision. "No," she uttered again, slapping her head to clear the muddle of fog it had become. "No," she said more firmly. "29Zebra—dial 911. Do it now!"

She felt a flicker of hope when she heard the synthetic ringtone on the other end, but those hopes collapsed when the ringtone abruptly cut out. "29Zebra, what happened?"

"Your call did not go through."

"Ohmygod." Fresh tears streaked the dust on her cheeks. She trembled at the unreality of her situation, then barked an order with all her strength.

"*Try again, dammit!*"

This time the ring-tone was scratchy, cutting in and out, and the voice on the other end was so broken that Ainsley couldn't tell if it was a man or woman let alone what the person was saying. "Hello? Can you hear me? Hello?" A dial tone clicked in with deadly finality.

"Your call was disconnected," 29Zebra informed her dispassionately. "The signal strength appears to be weak in this area. I can try again in another location."

A crash through the brush along the trail behind her banished all thoughts of 911 and her disgust with 29Zebra. Ainsley ran. She ran for her life, directionless, and gave no thought to the branches that tore at her arms and face. She tasted iron on her lips, and salt, and dirt, and the slick mucus of terror. She lost the trail, plunged her arms through the woods as if she were swimming in a sea of thorns. The limned darkness became a distraction she could no longer endure, so she snatched the glasses from her face, took in the layered shadows with her natural vision, and in the featureless depths of the forest, knew that it was hopeless.

She collapsed in the dank hollow of a tree, pressed against it as the night pressed against her. Footfalls padded through the duff ahead, measured and carefully placed. A deep nasal growl came out of the dark, freezing her every muscle and trapping the breath in her throat. A pair of pale, luminescent eyes seemed to dance in the dark, coming closer ever so slowly until a face formed around them and it was the cougar.

Locked in a rictus against the tree, Ainsley took half gasps that passed no air over her lips. The cougar materialized as it padded closer, frightfully long, terrifyingly muscular, and with saliva dripping like blood from between the teeth of nightmares.

Ainsley meant to scream, but all that came out was a weak squeal at the bottom of each sharp, short breath. Her glasses were still clutched in her quivering hand. She raised them tremulously and pushed them over her eyes, where the cougar now appeared cuddly, a soft ball of warm fur to hug on a cold night.

Ainsley lowered her trembling arms, squeezed her eyes tightly, and then the cougar took her.

The professor shook off the self-pity and reminded himself that environmental sustainability, the subject of his class, was crucial to the future. None of his students, including Ainsley Beck Cohen-Dyer, was paying him the least attention, but if he could get through to just one of them, just one, then perhaps ecological disaster could still be averted. He nodded to himself and resumed his lecture.

"This cougar sighting is a case in point," he continued, "and not just the cougar, but all the species that have been displaced by the fires. Think about it. Driven into ever-smaller habitats, these species are now forced to compete outside of their instinctual niches for survival, creating stress and weaker offspring.

"Something not often considered but equally problematic is the crowding. Think of a dense urban slum, teeming with people who compete with one another at whatever level they are capable and with the prerogative of simple survival. This leads to broken traditions, to crime and violence, and yes, to disease. Now compare this to diminishing acreage in a degraded ecosystem and what you have are stressed species living in too-close proximity and lashing out violently, not for food as they would do in a behavioral norm, but for *space*. And then these same species, encountering other species that they would previously never have come in contact with, begin to spread disease among themselves, diseases to which they might never have been exposed, diseases like rabies, encephalopathy, and the ever-mutating coronavirus.

"Now imagine that cougar, an apex predator, fiercely territorial and definitely dangerous already, but what happens when it is hemmed into a shrinking habitat? It becomes stressed, frustrated—angry if you will. Always hungry, it is driven by necessity to hunt outside of its normal scope. Perhaps it has become diseased. Perhaps it is even rabid.

"That is not an animal I would want to encounter..."

THE
WORD

ASSOCIATE PROFESSOR DR. DARREN JAMISON realized in a startling instant of disbelief that his tenure prospects hung perilously on his next answer.

"I've never spoken that word in my life," he replied, disgusted by the defensive note in his voice, defensiveness that was completely unwarranted because what he'd said was completely true. He'd never used the word aloud. He loathed it in fact, so much so that when he encountered it in the literature he fought against even allowing a mental image to form. He stroked his russet Van Dyke, a nervous tick that was often interpreted as thoughtfulness by others. "It was in my paper, that's all. And I haven't even found a publisher yet."

The human resources counselor, Betny Carole, was probably Jamison's age or a little older, and wore her straight black hair in a severe cut that matched the tone of voice she was using with him. Jamison recognized her given name as a Norman-era English surname in one of its various spellings. He was professionally curious about how she had come to receive it as a first name, but the tense standoff he now found himself in did not invite a query along those lines.

Betny returned a sympathetically insincere smile and paused as if to frame her thoughts, although her retort was already on the tip of her tongue. She found Dr. Jamison to be an aloof man, average build, thirty-six years old, with wavy, reddish brown hair, and a mustache-goatee combination that belonged in old movies. He must be brilliant to be so close to tenure at his age and in the relatively obscure field of Comparative English Literature, and yet his attitude seemed medieval at best.

"Surely you recognize, Dr. Jamison, how offensive that word is, and how a student could be traumatized by seeing it."

"I am well aware of that, Ms. Carole, but—"

"There is no but to this," she cut in haughtily. "Published or not, an abstract of your paper was posted on your university page. You could as easily have used a euphemism and spared your students."

"What?" Jamison responded incredulously, heating around his collar. "If they can't read a controversial word in a scholarly paper then how can they read Twain or Faulkner, or Hemingway or Steinbeck, or...or even Baldwin or Wright?"

Her eyes rolled almost imperceptibly. "You know as well as I do that there is a lot of literature out there that avoids this completely. It is commensurate upon you to look out for the emotional well-being of your students."

Her words came in the egregiously disingenuous cadence of corporate-speak. When had the halls of higher consciousness become commercialized? Tenure had been created to guard against just this thing, and yet moneyed interests had still somehow slithered in. Jamison was shocked almost beyond endurance. "You can't be serious."

"I am very serious. You should take it that way, too."

"But I do!"

"I'm not sure I agree."

"Your agreement isn't relevant." He practically spat this.

"My agreement *is* relevant," she said tightly, "and so is your behavior."

Jamison went rigid at that veiled threat. This wasn't an open classroom debate, she held the pen and the papers and his future in whatever whim she felt. He took a cooling breath and settled back. "Look," he said in his calmest, most rational voice, "I do understand. In literature we touch on uncomfortable themes, and I do try to be as delicate as I can. If I could speak with the student who—"

She cut him off again and he could barely restrain himself. "You also know that complainants are entitled to anonymity," she said. "I can't reveal their identity under any circumstances, and as an associate professor applying for tenure you should support that."

"I do support that, but—"

"But what?"

There, dammit, she did it again.

"But—I mean—this isn't abuse or anything even remotely similar. One of my students was offended. I acknowledge that. If I could just speak with her—"

"Her?" Betny's dark brows arched at such a bald assumption.

He hadn't caught his error until it was already past his lips, and now, without a quick correction, he would have to banter with Betny about sexism as well. He sighed inwardly and appended, "Or him. Her or him."

Perhaps that awful genderless pronoun making the rounds had a place after all, even if the thought of using it made his stomach turn. There were so many innocuous traps these days, so many ways to offend people. Nevertheless, if he could only speak with his student—it took so little to elevate another human being, a smile, a compliment, a sincere expression of interest. If reason alone wouldn't do it, he was certain he could resolve this entire episode that simply.

"Well," Betny accepted his hasty addendum, albeit skeptically, "none of that matters anyway. You'll need to amend your paper, of course."

"Of course," Jamison agreed with a defeated sigh, although he wasn't sure how he would do it. He refused to use a pathetic euphemism to gloss over an ugly reality, or consign the greatest authors of an age to a dusty bookshelf only because their vernacular had preceded present sensibilities. But he would think on it, and he would find a way if that's what it took to protect his tenure.

"And you'll need to apologize."

"Apologize? What in God's name for?"

This time her eyes did roll and she meant for them to. "Dr. Jamison," she lectured, "you are simply refusing to take responsibility for yourself."

"But I haven't done anything to take responsibility for."

"And your refusal to accept that," she came right back, "is further proof of your culpability."

He couldn't endure this a moment longer. "That's patently circular, *Ms. Carole.*" He spat her name as if it were something foul on his tongue.

"That's reality, *Associate* Professor Jamison," she spat in return.

Both fell back in their chairs as if weary of battle. Jamison rubbed at an incipient headache. "So what, then?" he asked after a moment.

"Unless you're prepared to formally apologize, you'll have to appear before the disciplinary committee."

Jamison groaned, his mind working through a chessboard of outcomes. If he apologized, he would be capitulating to the most absurdly closed-minded complaint imaginable, which would then force him to dilute his course plan into a lazy study of only the most contemporarily inoffensive material, while if he went before the disciplinary committee his tenure would dangle in even greater jeopardy. He was still relatively young, but starting over at another university would reset the clock. He wouldn't make tenure in his lifetime, but would instead probably wind up in a public school system trying to teach incurious kids why it was important to introduce similes properly. His anger flared and he squeezed a fist to keep it in check.

"So you mean one of those disingenuous apologies that politicians and football players use all the time," he offered flippantly, "such as 'I'm sorry that someone was offended by reading a word they didn't like.' That kind of apology?"

Betny could no longer conceal her contempt. It showed in a squint and pressed lips, and a cheek that trembled ever so slightly. Her nostrils were flaring, so taut was her expression. "You will need," she dictated in measured breaths, "to offer a sincere public apology."

She'd finally found his limit and had bulled right on through it. "I'll go before the committee, then," he said stonily. There would be at least a few tenured professors on the committee. They would understand, surely they would.

"If that's the way you want it," Betny said piteously. She flipped a folder closed, and then with an icy glare, invited him to leave.

Jamison lived alone in a studio apartment beyond the frat houses east of campus. He walked past those frat houses twice a day, often heard the partying inside, often saw the evidence on the lawns: empty alcohol containers, draperies of toilet paper, male and female students in various stages of undress passed out on the porches—as bacchanalian as Greek life could be. He no longer shook his head when he went past. He had a duty to report their behavior, but futility in the face of moneyed intransigence would serve no one's interests. Greek life persisted to give these kids the childhoods they hadn't had when they were children.

He stepped up into his apartment wearily, flipped on the lights, and lingered in his doorway, pondering. He had no love interest at the moment. In fact, he'd had no love interest for a while now. Focused so firmly on his career, there wasn't enough emotional room remaining to develop anything that would endure, which would be as unfair to a partner as it would be to himself. With tenure would come time for emotional attachments. It's what he'd been working toward all his adult life, and the reality of it was close, so close.

He had cancelled his last class that day, not only because he had been so dismasted by the events in the human resources office, but also because his social media was erupting with the vilest comments. One revolting word had set this in motion, and yet words as equally revolting were being hurled at him with no sense whatsoever of the irony.

He recognized some of his students in the querulous queue, but most of his detractors appeared not to be associated with the university at all. Then he saw with horror that some right-wing group had taken up his defense, which then blew everything so wildly out of proportion that not even a kernel of truth remained. They vented only for the sake of venting, as if no other means existed to slake the angst in their lives. One small consolation was that at least the venom his students spat at him came in the form of complete sentences.

He could have handled this. He would have been more than willing—no, eager—to debate this with them in an academic setting, where even if tempers flared, even if agreement could not be reached, at least something could have been learned in the process. This online tirade, though, was senseless barbarity, a mob taking heads in the *Place de la Revolution* with neither forethought nor remorse nor any application of intellect.

He heeled his door closed, slumped onto his worn corduroy couch, and spent the next few minutes unpublishing his various social media pages. There was nothing he could do, though, about his university page, which was managed by the IT department; and they wouldn't take that page down without going through some overly bureaucratic process that would inflame the situation even further. How dare anyone, after all, attempt to censor the internet.

Tense days ran one into the next. Nothing moved quickly when it needed to. The disciplinary committee wouldn't convene for another week yet, and this as the momentum of self-righteous umbrage gathered force like an equatorial storm. Someone had painted *Racist* on his front door in dripping red paint. Students had been gathering in the quad in ever-greater numbers, holding up placards, lashing him with insults and jeers as he walked to his office. He had resolved to take a back route to his office from then on when the protest suddenly moved from the quad to the outskirts of campus, where right-wingers had set up a counter protest.

This new protest was thankfully across campus from his route to and from his apartment. He could have avoided it and been none the wiser, but morbid curiosity drew him there, discretely of course. The right-wingers were as obscenity-laced and obnoxious as the students. He shook his head in disgust. Some of the right-wingers looked like grizzled grandfathers. They were supposedly adults, although their behavior was indistinguishable from the least inhibited of the students.

Neither side heard anything; they had only moved their angst from the internet to the outdoors. The right-wingers were mostly white, mostly male, and mostly wearing red ball caps, while the students were evenly composed of male and female, although also mostly white. An intimidating line of vested and militarily-outfitted police in black uniforms worked with shields and truncheons to keep the two groups apart, more like soldiers holding off hordes of jihadis rather than civil servants keeping the peace. Galvanized barricades had been set up. The two sides were deadlocked in senseless diatribe. It was useless, futile, and profoundly undignified.

A few students had likened this to the movements of the 1960s. Jamison had studied the literature of that era, so knew that this disgrace was nothing of the sort. War and peace did not teeter in the balance here. The moral imperative was weak, and the participants were ignorant of everything but their insular little existences. Some of the right-wingers brandished signs promoting free speech. Jamison shook his head and resisted the urge to go forth and explain to them what free speech in the United States actually meant. It wouldn't have done any good. Nobody would have listened, and even if they had, they wouldn't have accepted his words.

He turned his back on the sorry scene and went to his office, where only one student was waiting to see him. Her name was Rashelle, she was black, and Jamison felt suddenly, desperately self-conscious.

"Hi Professor D," she greeted him cheerfully. "How are you getting on?" She disarmed him with a bright smile that eased the stiffness in his posture.

"You can imagine," he answered with his own smile, weak though it was. He ushered her to a seat, then took his own seat behind his desk. "So, what can I do for you?"

"I have some questions about your class yesterday."

Jamison gave her a pensive look. He'd cut back his classes because of the uproar, but simply refused to cancel them all. Despite this there had been few students in attendance. Rashelle had been one of them, perhaps the only one paying attention. The rest had worn indolent expressions and had seemed more interested in their phones.

"Questions?" he asked tentatively.

"Yeah, about the way racist words are embedded in English literature but don't necessarily imply racism, like instead they're a dramatic device. Man against man, you know, like Capulets and Montagues, or Jets and Sharks."

"Yes," he answered carefully. "Go on."

"I mean, it seems as if every culture on the planet has disparaging words they use for every other culture. Some are harmless enough, like the way the Brits call us Yanks, but others are pretty bad. And you're saying that none of this is racist?"

"No, not always. It is tribal, yes, but not necessarily to imply inferiority. These words are quite often used to define a competitive contrast, such as between the Capulets and Montagues. In order to compare and interpret literature from various periods, it's crucial that we understand this distinction or else the author's true meaning might be subsumed by modern prejudices."

Rashelle mulled that thoughtfully, her eyes seeming to search distantly for examples. Jamison gave her a moment and then continued:

"It's true that these words are used bluntly as racial slurs in some periods, but quite often in literature—and especially in English since it's an amalgam of so many other languages, and since the British Empire was so far-reaching and so recent in our history—we often see these words used without malice as regional adjectives. Think of Kipling, or the voyages of Captain Cook and the *Resolution*. For example, I could be described as a haole, honkey, paleface, or round-eye, and the reader would know immediately who the narrator is as well as the social setting and the time period, while casting me not in a racist sense but in a geographical and morphological sense. By using what are admittedly stereotypes, characterizations can be developed with an economy of words but not necessarily with racist implications."

"Hmm." Rashelle was still pondering deeply. She tapped her lip with a finger. "So if someone calls me—well, you know—then you're saying that's not racist?"

"No, Rashelle," he answered sadly. "If someone says that to you then he or she is a racist."

"But what if they're black and say it?"

"Then they're falling back on cultural indoctrination, not explicitly racist but derived from racial inequity. It's not a word I like to hear—from anybody."

"Why not?"

"Because that particular word is weighted with an ugly history no matter who speaks it."

"Yeah, I know, but still—I read it all the time. You can't get through the eighteenth and nineteenth centuries and not see it everywhere. I used to get so upset, but now sometimes I see it and it doesn't seem to mean anything different than...well, than Capulet or Montague."

"That's what I've been trying to demonstrate, but I'm still not comfortable with that word. Sure, someone could just be socially inept and not necessarily a racist, but our culture has caught up with an associative interpretation and the word should be avoided regardless. My argument is only that authors of earlier eras were not necessarily using it the way we interpret it today, and that we shouldn't be offended by it or assume anything out of context."

"So you're saying Mark Twain wasn't racist?"

Jamison smiled wanly. This was an old argument in academic circles. "He was no more racist than any other author using the vernacular of his time. There were other words of that era he could have used if he'd definitely intended to imply racism."

"Such as what?"

"I won't say them aloud, Rashelle."

"If you're willing to bring them up, then why not? Are you so sensitive because you're from South Africa?"

Jamison met her eyes with a start, but quickly decided from her earnest expression that she wasn't trying to imply something by association. "I was born in South Africa," he explained, and not for the first time, "but I was raised here. That has nothing to do with the way I feel. There are words in Afrikaans that are directly proportional, and I don't use them either. If you want to know even uglier words from the nineteenth century, the words Twain and others could have used, you can find them on your own with a little research."

"I hear you, Professor D." Rashelle stood with an appreciative smile. "Thanks for talking with me." She turned to leave but then paused. "And all of this that's goin' on?" She twirled a finger in the air and grinned. "You hang in there."

"Thank you, Rashelle," he exhaled, relieved that the conversation was over but glad it had occurred just the same. One more week—with students like Rashelle, he might make it yet.

The week wouldn't wait. The IT department moved with sudden and uncharacteristic alacrity to remove his university page, which was a harbinger of the dispassionate email he received later that evening announcing his suspension pending the outcome of his disciplinary hearing. Jamison berated himself for not seeing this coming. A tenured professor would have been politely asked, in an in-person visit from a deferential department head, to take a well-earned sabbatical while passions calmed, but without tenure he was as expendable as a clipped fingernail.

Even more galling was that a student teacher had been assigned to take over his classes, delegitimizing his work and meaning that at least one more person would be spending the entire period poking at a phone. Jamison was told to stay off campus until his hearing, not because of any disruptions this might cause but because the entire football team had refused to play that weekend otherwise.

Jamison languished in his apartment as the days passed, feeling more alone than that day in Johannesburg when his parents had been killed. His only sibling, an older sister named Ruby who had already moved out on her own when this happened, had been unreachable. What followed had been bewildering days of displacement, abandonment, and staggering loneliness, making Nelson Mandela's ascension to the presidency seem insignificant in the interim. Jamison had eventually been taken in by jubilant people with infectious smiles, people he had been kept apart from throughout his short life, people who had previously existed to him in only the most abstract way, and people who were profoundly different from everything he had ever known.

They treated him kindly. He didn't learn until much later that he'd had no right to expect such compassion from them, and when that knowledge came it brought with it residual feelings of complicity that he had never fully reconciled. Ruby caught up with him by and by, and after confronting his foster family with words and accusations that sickened him with shame, she took her brother and emigrated to America. Ruby got them settled, and then, as if inconvenienced by her new responsibilities, moved on with her embittered life. The two weren't close, so Ruby was no one he would call on for comfort. As again on that Johannesburg street, he felt bewildered and alone.

He did not endure this condition for long. A thought lodged and grew, drawing a quiet smile from contemplative lips. His paper was itself his best, most competent defense! True, the subject of his paper was controversial, or rather, the supporting evidence was controversial, but he'd spent years refining his argument. His ideas were sound regardless how they were perceived, so he would go boldly before the disciplinary committee, to defend not only his dream of tenure but his life's work as well!

By Monday morning, the protestors on both sides had mostly filtered off in search of more stimulating fare, although tensions still simmered. A few students noted his passage with acid glares between glances at their phones, but none confronted him. The football team had lost the game on Saturday, which had roused enough emotion to displace other passions.

The day was warm and clear with a hint of humidity, but despite this he wore his tweed jacket with the leather elbow patches. Along with khakis and suede loafers, he projected the stereotypical air of comfortable academia, not far removed from how he felt. He was as confidant now as when his radical idea had first taken root. If the result was that he would soon be teaching in a thankless public school, then so be it.

The hearing was held in the meeting room down the hall from Betny's office. Her door was closed as he went by, which drew a sigh of relief. Betny Carole evoked in him a loathing that he couldn't quite define, so hers was a face he could just as well do without on a day like this. It didn't occur to him until he walked into the meeting room that Betny might have been called in, and there she was, her lips tightened judgmentally. It wasn't that he feared her presence, only that she had already demonstrated that no argument would sway her. At some point in her career she had allowed herself to become inured in a rigid corporate mindset, as immutable as a handprint in cement. He could only hope that the other committee members would be more receptive.

The committee was ridiculously large, crowded behind three folding tables that had been adjoined in order to accommodate them all, and bordered with stakeholders who had only the most tenuous connection to the issue. The university's provost chaired the committee. Jamison didn't know him personally. The provost was not a scholarly man, but was instead an administrative apparatchik apparently sitting in for the president, who was probably off somewhere flirting and fundraising. The dean of the English department sat to the provost's right. Jamison and the dean had a cordial relationship, although strictly professional. Positioned on either side of them were the tenured professors. Jamison was on friendly terms with some of them, others, made obvious by their frowns, were less supportive. On the wings of the long table were a student representative—just a kid from Jamison's perspective, but inflated importance had gotten him in—and a few lay people from the community presumably brought in for the sake of transparency. There was only one black person attending, a middle-aged woman with a noble frosting of gray in her hair. Jamison had no idea who she was.

Jamison took a lonely seat behind a small wooden table whose varnish had been worn away where his elbows rested. He had been provided with a legal pad and pen, and a plastic bottle of water. He eased the wasteful plastic bottle distastefully aside with an index finger. He wouldn't need the pad and pen. There was also a microphone, which he didn't think he would need either. The provost gaveled the hearing to order.

"We are here," the provost announced into his microphone, which reverberated painfully with feedback. He cleared a disconcerted throat, warily pushed the microphone aside as if it might nip his fingers, and began again. "We are here to review the use of inappropriate racial slurs—"

Jamison's hand shot up, which threw the provost off his prepared remarks and drew a discomfited frown. "Slur, sir," Jamison said. "Only the one. Not plural."

"I think," one of the less friendly professors spoke up, "we will find that this is not the case, but that you have engaged in a pattern of—"

"Oh, let it go, Chuck," the dean interjected. The dean's name was Dr. William Carlyle, and while he and Jamison were not especially close, he was not a man to suffer aggrandizing fools. "We're here for the one issue, not your objections to Dr. Jamison's thesis. I move that we focus only on the issue in question."

"Second," someone said in a bored voice.

"Very well," said the provost. "Slur, then. The manual of conduct clearly states that the word in question is inflammatory, grossly insensitive, and will not be used in any capacity."

Jamison's hand shot up again. "Applied, sir," he said.

"What's that?"

"Applied, sir. The manual of conduct states that the word will not be *applied* in any capacity, clearly indicating that the word is not to be used in reference to any person, whether student body or faculty; that such application would constitute a hostile environment."

"That's pure semantics, Dr. Jamison," the provost grumbled.

"Semantics is what we do in the English department, sir," Jamison managed to say with a straight face.

The provost hesitated as if he had missed a punch line; then, "Very well. But you did *apply* it in your paper, did you not?"

"No, sir. I *referenced* it."

Dr. Carlyle smiled imperceptibly, while the provost seemed flustered.

"I don't know that such a small distinction has any bearing here," the provost countered after a moment of confusion.

"Quite the contrary, sir," Jamison rebutted. "We choose our words carefully for just this reason." Jamison beamed, albeit inwardly. Betny, he noticed, was scowling.

"Uh, well I uh..." the provost stammered.

"Perhaps we have overlooked the introductions?" Dr. Carlyle suggested quietly to the provost.

"Uh, yes, of course, dean. Please go ahead."

"Dr. Jamison," Dr. Carlyle said, mirth still glinting in his eyes, "you know most of the people here, and they know you. Others will need introduction. To my far right is Miriam Hill." He was referring to the black woman. "She chairs the governor's equal opportunity commission. To her left is Chris Laine representing the student government." Chris wore the hostile expression of the protest line. "And on my far left is Betny Carole of Human Resources. I believe you already know each other."

Jamison nodded, while Betny crossed her arms tightly and glowered.

"There are others here purely as observers," Dr. Carlyle continued, "so I don't think those introductions need to be made. For the purposes of the record, Dr. Jamison, you are currently an associate professor?"

"Yes, associate professor of Comparative English Literature."

"And what are your credentials?"

"I hold a master's in Comparative English and a doctorate in Linguistics."

"Impressive. And what is the title of the paper that has caused all of this consternation?"

"Semantic Drift by Means of Applied Social Stigmatization."

To Jamison's surprise, Dr. Carlyle gave him a discreet wink. "Hmm, quite ambitious. Well, that takes care of the introductions, but I'd like to ask a few questions if I may."

"Go ahead," Jamison and the provost assented simultaneously. The provost grumbled at the confusion, while Jamison maintained a bland expression. Dr. Carlyle continued:

"You are fluent in both Latin and French?"

"I am, and with a functional knowledge of German, Gaelic, and Norse."

"Of course," Dr. Carlyle nodded. "The roots of the language."

"And Afrikaans," Miriam Hill interjected loudly. Jamison was startled to hear from that end of the table.

"Uh, yes, and Afrikaans," he answered with a confused dip of brows.

"Why didn't you mention that, too?" she asked accusingly. Jamison was not flustered.

"Because Afrikaans is not a root of the English language and has no bearing on my research."

"But you are South African, are you not?"

"No, ma'am. I'm a naturalized American citizen."

"But you were born in South Africa?"

"Yes, ma'am."

"Under Apartheid?"

"Yes, ma'am."

"Your parents were murdered, weren't they?"

"Ms. Hill!" Dr. Carlyle objected. "That is a sensitive and personal topic, and this is not a court of law."

"I merely wish this committee to understand Dr. Jamison's complete history," she countered.

"It's quite all right," Jamison offered. "I don't mind answering Ms. Hill's questions."

"Very good," Ms. Hill said. Her expression was carefully contained, neither belligerent nor beneficent. "And, Dr. Jamison, your parents were murdered by a..."

She trailed off knowingly, and Jamison knew why. Her questions were meant to shake him, but they didn't and they wouldn't. He was certain that she was attempting to endow him with the most base of motivations, but those motivations simply didn't exist.

"A black man, yes, Ms. Hill."

"So it's not unreasonable," she went on, "that this experience might, uhm, *influence* your perspective somewhat."

"No," Jamison retorted immediately, "or rather, yes—it is unreasonable. I was just a boy when it happened. I had no experience with racial recrimination. Children seldom exhibit those propensities unless they've been indoctrinated by their parents, and I wasn't."

Antithetical to her line of questioning, Miriam Hill seemed pleased by Jamison's response. She turned to Dr. Carlyle. "That's all I have for now," she said.

"Very well." Dr. Carlyle was visibly disturbed by the direction the questioning had taken. "I now yield to the chair."

"Thank you, dean," the provost said. "So now, uhm, the matter of the paper. Dr. Jamison, you used, uhm—well, this is indelicate, but you, uhm, alluded to a racial epithet in your paper, didn't you?"

"No, sir. I used the actual word."

"Then why don't you just say it aloud?" Chuck, the truculent professor, groused. Jamison held up a hand to mask an incipient smile. After Dr. Carlyle's earlier intervention, Jamison could now only think of this imperious man as *Dr. Chuck.*

"Because it's a uniquely harmful word with an ugly history," Jamison explained.

"And yet you used it in your paper."

"Of course. It's a word in the language. Where else could we discuss its evolution?"

"With its vile history, I would be inclined to purge it completely."

"Then would you also purge Mark Twain, one of the greatest authors in American letters?"

"Twain is overrated, Dr. Jamison," Dr. Chuck said donnishly, which drew a muffled gasp from somewhere in the group.

"I beg to disagree, and Twain isn't the only author you would have to purge. You would, essentially, have to purge two centuries of literature."

"I'm not saying that," Dr. Chuck reacted angrily. "A prudent dissection would serve the purpose."

"A prudent censoring, you mean."

"Don't put words in my mouth, Dr. Jamison, and don't be so disingenuous. You know as well as I that there is ample literature of that period which avoids this controversy completely." Betny smiled thinly in support of that statement.

"Yes, that's true, but perhaps the greatest of it would be, under your regime, strictly off limits, and I believe to our detriment. Not only would literature be impacted, but history as well."

"History? How so?" Dr. Chuck asked skeptically.

"Well, consider an historian attempting to interpret the nineteenth century with no knowledge of *Huckleberry Finn* or *Life on the Mississippi.* It's unimaginable."

"You are cleverly over-inflating the issue, Dr. Jamison. Your argument does not hold." Dr. Chuck had become so animated that he had cowed the others into stunned silence, with the exception of Dr. Carlyle, who was listening closely and with intent. "It is neither immoral nor unethical to emplace a substitution for the offensive word."

Jamison was prepared for this. It was, after all, the focus of his work. "Dr.—" Jamison almost said Dr. *Chuck*, but caught himself in time. "—substituting a euphemism for an unacceptable word will eventually create an unacceptable euphemism, which will then be replaced by another word or euphemism that will itself eventually become unacceptable in an unending cycle of word substitution for the purpose of easing contemporary sensibilities."

Dr. Chuck opened his mouth to object, but Jamison pressed on. "Furthermore, the action you prescribe takes useful words out of circulation, allowing other perfectly acceptable words to eventually be shunned due to misdirected sensibilities, only to have themselves then taken out of circulation or else replaced with forced or entirely inelegant combinations of words. Attempting to police a language is ridiculous as well as futile, while turning our backs on a thousand years of scholarship and refinement is shameful."

Dr. Carlyle looked down to hide a smile that he could not control, while Dr. Chuck gaped. Some of the tenured professors hid their own smiles, while others reflected Dr. Chuck's incomprehension. The provost was simply befuddled, Betny had rolled her eyes at the ceiling, and Chris was looking dazed, his mouth hanging open. The lay people were simply lost. Miriam Hill, however, had her chin propped thoughtfully on a thumb.

It took Dr. Chuck a moment to find his voice. His eyes darted left and right in search of a learned rebuttal, but all he could come up with was, "That's a bold statement. What's your evidence?"

"Faggot," Jamison answered stunningly. Gasps emanated.

"Wha—what did you just say?" Dr. Chuck asked in shock.

"Faggot," Jamison answered again, "from the Old French, derived from *fagotter*, meaning one who makes bundles of firewood. The word became associated with the burning of heretics and then evolved into an abusive term applied to, among others, homosexuals. It became an acceptable epithet over time. It was even embraced for a period, but was then rejected by contemporary sensibilities and replaced with queer, an adjective from Old High German that means perverse or odd, converted into a noun in the early twentieth century, again referring to homosexuals, again embraced for a period, and again replaced by contemporary sensibilities with gay, another adjective from Old French that means joyous and carefree and was adapted in the United States via prison slang to mean homosexual. Gay is the currently accepted substitute for homosexual but you can be sure that it, too, will be replaced eventually."

"And what is your point?" Dr. Chuck asked, aghast.

"My point is that the word homosexual is as inoffensive as the word heterosexual, while queer and gay have all but been banished from our modern lexicon despite the utility of their proper definitions. Readers of literature prior to the twentieth century will encounter these words quite often, where the words serve a succinct purpose that we cannot achieve similarly today with any brevity. And while an English soldier might throw a faggot on Joan of Arc's pyre, throwing a bundle of wood on that same pyre sounds inelegant and out of period. No modern author, however, would dare describe throwing a faggot on a pyre without first expending a few additional words of explanation."

Jamison sat back and took a breath, while Dr. Chuck struggled in frustration for a rebuttal that he felt should have come easily. "So what you're suggesting," he finally decided, "is that we all use disparaging slurs at will?"

"Not at all, and for the same reason that we don't use profanity in elevated conversation, because profanity is inelegant and belies a greater mastery of vocabulary. The use of profanity, though, does not lead to universal condemnation and social retribution."

"I still cannot grasp your point. It would seem that you believe language should be frozen at some time period prior to now."

"Of course not. Words change meaning or take on additional meanings for a variety of reasons. Sometimes accents will cause the mispronunciation of a word, which then establishes itself over time; and sometimes the speaker doesn't know the proper definition of a word, establishing with use a secondary definition. Some words are metaphorically redefined by slang. Others are modified for rhyme or meter and are then disseminated through popular culture. But in our modern social sense we see the conscious replacement of perfectly acceptable words with others that sound more soothing to the present generation. This is socially stigmatized language change as opposed to organically or academically driven language change."

"So what's wrong with that?"

"Nothing, beyond pillaging perfectly practical words to assuage overly sensitive sensibilities."

"So you are defining which words people should and should not be able to use?"

"No, that's what you're doing. I'm only documenting the change and offering an interpretation of the cause."

There were enough heads nodding to give Jamison a note of confidence. Dr. Carlyle was now smiling and not trying to hide it. Miriam Hill remained unreadable, while Chris looked as if he'd had an epiphany. The provost looked no less befuddled, and Dr. Chuck was going purple with outrage. Betny was stone, but that was to be expected.

"So what, then, Dr. Jamison?" Dr. Chuck spat in indignation. "Are we to set aside a cadre of words for use among only certain groups of people? Because that's what it sounds like to me."

Jamison sighed. He was of the opinion that sequestering words for acceptable use only within certain groups was itself racist, not to mention thoroughly divisive. If left unchecked, a white author would be vilified for writing about black characters, and vice versa. Jamison had already seen minor examples of this in the making. This attitude could soon migrate to genders as well, balkanizing the language beyond common understanding. He felt the same about hyphenated ethnic origins, but that was an issue for the sociology department to deal with.

"No," Jamison explained with a pained look, "that's not the solution, but neither is purging offensive language from the lexicon."

"Then we do nothing, is that what you're saying? That we should actually endorse the rampant use of abusive language? Because I don't see any other alternative."

"There is an alternative, professor, but first we have to accept that there is no period in history, or people populating it, that hasn't experienced brutal persecution; no people who haven't at some point suffered indignity and powerlessness and felt the sting of coined epithets. At the same time, we have to accept that cleansing the language won't absolve history, and there are lessons in that history that we must not lose."

Jamison took a breath. This next was his final argument and he had to get it right.

"These words exist. Language will change, that is inevitable, but it is incumbent upon us to document and if possible moderate that change; and we do that by presenting students with words, the origin and history of those words, and how those words have evolved, not by denying the existence of those words in the first place.

"Institutions of higher learning set the standard for all of education. It is therefore also incumbent upon us to be willing to engage in open dialogue on these issues without fear of reprisal, because if we won't then nobody will and our language will veer away from scholarly advancement and descend into pidgin. Why else do we have a Department of English?"

Dr. Chuck remained unimpressed. "That was a wonderful speech, Dr. Jamison, but you still offer no solution to the problem."

"That's because no solution exists beyond simple decorum. Decorum begins with us and then trickles throughout our educational system. Decorum is not aversion, and decorum is not denial. Decorum is the learned practice of language."

Dr. Chuck smirked contemptuously. "Be polite, then? Really? That's your learned solution? So it follows that if we're not always on our best behavior then we must be racists?"

Jamison shook his head sadly. Institutionalized thinking is what created the barriers, not people in general. "We don't always mean to be," he said, "but without a common language and a common literature we will always seem to be."

Miriam Hill slapped her palm twice on the table, drawing every eye, and in some of those eyes the fear that some irredeemable insult had occurred. She stood with measured dignity, sternly meeting the gazes around her but then settling her unsettling focus on Dr. Chuck. She held that look a blink longer than was comfortable for him, and then said in a voice that carried firmly from one end of the table to the other, "As the sole—and curiously, I might add—person of color on this panel, I must say that I agree completely with Dr. Jamison. No amount of scholarly handwringing will absolve history of what my people have suffered at the hands of man or the venom of his words, and to deny that fact serves nothing more than to sooth guilty consciences.

"I have seen and heard enough, and what I have seen and heard is both hopeful and disturbing. I have no vote in these proceedings, so I can only encourage you to make the right decision. Thank you."

She sat amid a weighted silence that defied any rebuttal or comment. The provost looked acutely uncomfortable, while Dr. Chuck's jaw hung speechless. Betny had shifted her stony expression to her hands, which were clenched white. Dr. Carlyle nodded thoughtfully and flicked a glance at Jamison, who displayed no outward sign of surprise or shock or even relief.

Dr. Carlyle cleared his throat before addressing the provost. "I believe there are no more arguments to be made. Perhaps we can move to a vote now?"

"Uh, uh, yes," the provost said unsteadily, as if still coming to grips with what he'd heard. "Without objection we'll move to the vote."

"No objection," someone said."

"Very well." The provost turned his attention toward Jamison. "If you could wait outside, Dr. Jamison, we'll deliberate and call you back when we're ready."

"Yes, sir." Jamison stood. "Thank you."

Jamison sat on a hard wooden bench outside the meeting room door, unconfident how the vote would go and wondering how he might be received were he to return to South Africa. Probably not well, he decided. His accent had become Americanized. He wouldn't fit in. The door opened and Chris came out.

"I thought your argument was brilliant, Professor," Chris practically gushed, quite a change from his earlier expression. "I never thought about it that way."

Jamison looked wan, his fingers laced on his knees. He smiled weakly. "Thank you."

"I'd like to get into one of your classes next term."

Jamison looked up in surprise. "The way things stand, I don't know if you'll get that opportunity."

"Well I hope so, anyway. Good luck, Professor."

Chris left then, up the hallway past Betny's office and then out into the sunlit day. Jamison's thoughts ranged through every word of his defense, weighing them, reorganizing them, looking for combinations that might have had more impact. He had possibly swayed Miriam Hill, and Dr. Carlyle seemed supportive, but Dr. Chuck wouldn't have been convinced, or those professors who clung to Dr. Chuck as if he were an academic messiah.

Minutes passed as he dwelled on these thoughts, his tenure, his argument, his very future out of his hands. The door banged open and Betny came out. She looked at him with her usual disdain, an expression that even an earthquake wouldn't dislodge. "They want you inside," she announced as if reluctantly, and then she turned abruptly and went back in.

Jamison rose woodenly, ran fingers through his hair, and went in to find out what his future would be.

KINGDOM SPRING

KINGDOM SPRING was a mountain village settled in a bowl between heavenly peaks whose slopes were as fertile as Eden.

The pioneer fathers had wrested it from the Indians in a bloodletting that was still commemorated early each summer, when the ladies wore their brightest whites, the men their stiffest blacks, the children attired in miniature, and all met at the spring that lent the village its name; for there the pioneer fathers had stumbled upon the purest fount of water, which gurgled cold and clean directly from the mossy ground and flowed a short distance into a deep cerulean pool among trees that stood as tall and wide as the pyramids of gospel. It was a holy place meant for the chosen, who had paid its price in blood and gristle.

The villagers gathered on that sultry morning, hand in hand around the pool, to pay homage and drink of the healing waters. Preacher Prine stood in his black, as erect as the mighty trees that once grew plentiful and now formed houses and church and sundry other edifices, as well as a sawmill that was famous in counties all around for its peerless lumber.

Billy Bailey toed the grass in his too-tight patent leather shoes. It was a growing spurt, his mother told him, but the shoes must be made to last at least one more season. He tugged at his confining collar and wiggled his cramped toes as Preacher Prine, already beading sweat above his handsome brows, held his dog-eared bible aloft and extolled the virtues of the pioneer fathers.

The resemblance many of the young ones bore to Preacher Prine was disregarded as either a coincidence of nature or nurture; but what every woman in the settlement knew—and no man but one imagined—was that the Prines had always been randy rascals, prowling the parlors of the parish with alacrity while the men were off laboring in the fields. And that was the core of Preacher Prine's problem. Too many of the youngsters were too closely related to eventually marry and beget the next generation, a condition of which the youngsters and their fathers were quite unaware, leaving the women wringing their hands in worry because, as all knew, young love could not be denied. Accidents would eventually occur, not to mention the queasy knowledge half the village held of imminent incest in their midst.

It was Preacher Prine's grandfather, Pressfield Prine, who had conjured the solution that nipped the tragedy of illicit love in the bud of its blossoming. Boys of a certain resemblance, on their thirteenth birthdays, were baptized among much ceremony in the holy waters of Kingdom Spring, then banished into the world to spread the righteous word and sow whatever wild oats they might gather. Those paltry few who returned years later inevitably did so holding the hands of fresh new brides who would birth new blood before, also inevitably, a Prine would come to call.

The girls received a similar baptism on their thirteenth birthdays, but their reward was to be made wives to the boys Prine chose for them (he kept meticulous breeding records between the pages of his dog-eared bible), which was immediately ordained before the congregation amid much expostulation toward the heavens, although strictly unconsummated until the time was propitious. Girls and mothers would cry, boys would tip taller in their tight shoes and grin wide in anticipation, while fathers, with lips aquiver, would take a sudden interest in the toes of their own shoes. When proper matches could not be made (and none but the women—and of course Prine—understood the mystery of this), girls were pressed into trades—sowing, cleaning, milling, baking &c.—and when *their* moments were propitious a Prine would call on them, caringly if disingenuously counsel them, and sometimes, among the fairer complected, employ them in his home for a time.

It was an ingenious plan with multitudinous manifestations for the Prines, but still insufficient to forestall the feared eventuality. Billy Bailey, a freckled redhead with clever green eyes who had turned thirteen years old that day, was blissfully unaware of Prine's problem and, although Billy had no idea just yet, was crucial to the survival of the settlement. The women in Billy's line were a dowdy lot who had, throughout the settlement's history, attracted the affections of only the most desperately afflicted. No Prine had visited those parlors, and so Billy was pure to husband among any of the girls present.

Which was yet another problem for Prine because Billy was a handful. Prine always wondered if somehow the boy knew, somewhere deep in his blood, that he occupied this place of exalted importance, protected from punishment by the pernicious presence of his undisparaged seed. Billy was willful, a prankster who paraded a perturbing panoply of provocation wherever he placed his feet. His latest escapade was the eggs, spirited from the hens in the dead of night, sucked of their contents and refilled with water (by means that remained a mystery to all those who pondered it), which splattered with sizzling and arresting suddenness when cracked into the hot grease of breakfast pans.

A dozen or more eggs suffered this fate, with a dozen or more fingers burned, the perpetrator known to all but proved by none, and this while Billy lay lethargically in his bed, clutching his distended belly and with a sallow look on his face. There had been consternation aplenty, and remonstrances to Prine, who could only force a tight smile onto frowning lips and label it the waywardness of youth. It was always a precarious balance maintaining his authority over them while also projecting the visage of friend, confidant, and spiritual advisor. The boy's baptism would come by and by, he argued, which assuaged the villagers for the time being, although Prine understood that this would only be a temporary remedy. What to do about the boy continued to vex him.

Billy's mother Adine, plain in the face, with lifeless hair, heavy brows, dull eyes, and sharper in the mind than she ever let on, also worried about her boy, although his ability to antagonize Prine did fill her with a certain pride. Nevertheless the boy could still go too far and find himself banished with the rest if he weren't careful. How to remedy this was her constant companion.

"Billy," she would say, patting down the cowlick that defied spit, water, and even grease. "You must stop these pranks."

"What pranks, Mama?" he would mouth innocently, to which she would shake her head wearily and sigh.

"He'll send you away, boy."

"I'm not afraid of Preacher Prine. And besides, he's gonna do that anyway."

She beamed inwardly but kept it tightly concealed. If only her husband were so bold, and if only her son knew how special he was. "Just be very careful," she said after that moment of introspection.

"I will, Mama. I promise." He said this with a mischievous smirk that his mother did not notice.

Preacher Prine first became aware of Billy Bailey (in a more than abstract sense) five years earlier when Prine was escalading the soon to be widowed Mrs. May in an aerie four-poster bed beneath a sunny window that overlooked the sawmill and the soon to be deceased Mr. May hard at work therein. Billy was not especially fond of Mrs. May, who mouthed gossip like a songbird and had the annoying habit of twisting his ear whenever Billy veered too close.

"You are a scoundrel, Billy Bailey," she would crow, this because Billy had dug up all the bright tulips in her flower garden and had then replanted them upside down, blooms in the soil and bulbs lopsided on their stems in the sun; and this because Mrs. May had, with an unwarranted scowl, swept the dust from her porch onto the boy when he ambled by one day and failed to offer her the proper deference. She had no proof that Billy had violated her tulips, of course, but she knew a mischievous malcontent when she saw one.

The persecution that followed was intolerable for Billy, which is why on one particular day—having managed to evade school (a relief to his teacher, it must be said) by means of a bout of gas that he could release at will as a staccato drumroll or, with a discreet shift of cheeks, a piercing whistle or, for stealth and amusement, a silent malodor—Billy was lying flat on Mrs. May's steep shaker-shingled roof and peering over the side into that sunlit window.

What he saw was damned peculiar. Mrs. May was on her knees, on her bed, bent over and clutching the headboard with both hands, her skirts billowing around her hips as Preacher Prine, dressed all in black as usual, his face strained red and with the cords standing out in his neck, was pounding his hips into those billowing skirts with the frenetic restlessness of a rabbit. Billy had never seen this kind of thing, wasn't sure what the two were doing, but there was something illicit about it that intrigued him.

So he made himself comfortable under the bluest sky, the air still crisp from a lingering winter, and watched the show, which was over in a disappointing moment. Preacher Prine was wrestling with his trousers then, whatever he had been up to still concealed by those billowing skirts, and that was when Mr. May looked up from his work at the saw-mill and saw Billy lying on his roof.

"Get down from there you fool!" Mr. May hollered, startling Billy, who slid an inch or so toward oblivion before managing to catch himself. Mr. May was loping toward the house now, and Billy saw disaster in the making. He pushed himself backward on the rotting shingles, broke a few loose, slipped some more, then bumped and kicked for purchase, which alerted Preacher Prine and the soon to be widowed Mrs. May below. Prine, clutching his open trousers, made a run for the back stairs as Mr. May took the front stairs two at a time and burst into the room, where he found his wife, hair akimbo, patting frantically at her skirts and with her stockings gathered like loose skin around her ankles.

Just then the backdoor boomed and, with a last despairing look at his wife, Mr. May bolted for the back stairs. He caught a toe on the carpet runner and toppled end over end to the lower landing, where he lay still with glazed eyes, his neck at an odd angle. Preacher Prine made it across the backyard in four long strides, leapt the fence and, risking a glance over his shoulder for a pursuer, spotted Billy Bailey coming down the trellis on the side of the house. That was all he had time to see—not knowing that Mrs. May was now a widow—for, assuming a painful predicament to follow, he was again running for his life.

Mrs. May steered away from gossip after that day, Mr. May was buried with adequate demonstrations of grief, and Preacher Prine kept a cool albeit caustic eye on Billy Bailey from thereon.

When he was ten, Billy by chance discovered the entrance to a cave under the massive stump of a once-proud chestnut whose exposed and rotting roots wrapped around a large moss-covered rock like the tentacles of an octopus.

What had preceded this discovery was another discovery in the shed behind Wilson's Apothecary, where gallon casks of Wilson's Distilled Elixir (another famous feature of Kingdom Spring) awaited transport to the appreciative farther regions. Wilson's Distilled Elixir was heralded as a miracle cure for myriad maladies, from ague to alimentary ailments, not to mention languor and lethargy, conditions that sounded wildly exotic to Billy, and so he was intrigued.

Swiveling an outside board on its single rusty nail (a strategic modification that Billy had replicated in walls and fences throughout Kingdom Spring), Billy slipped into the shed for a closer look. The casks were sealed with wooden plugs that simply refused to come loose, so in frustration Billy took a hammer to one, and after a couple of swings succeeded in knocking the plug into the liquid within, which sloshed a considerable amount of the venerated elixir onto his hands and feet. He took a smell and a taste and scowled, for the astringent liquid seemed no different than what his mother used on his cuts and scratches, a torture he perennially dreaded now that he was older and wiser; and worse yet, someone was rattling the lock outside.

Being caught in flagrante (a great word he learned from a salacious book he purloined from his prim teacher's desk) would go against form, and yet here was the punctured cask poised to provide evidence. With quick action, Billy spirited the cask and himself through the wall and into the alley beyond, pausing only long enough to listen for shouts of consternation, which did not come, so he was in the clear and could now take his time disposing of the evidence, which became a glaring problem the moment he stepped into the street.

There were people out and about, and he not in school but with a sloshing cask in his arms. He ducked back into the alley, spied the water trough in front of the livery, then grinned. Carefully timing the comings and goings of the village folk, he sprinted out of the alley, poured the glugging contents into the trough, then rolled the empty cask back into the alley. Wiping his hands on his pants, he made momentary eye contact with the single mule at the trough, which lowered its insouciant gaze and began lapping at the water. Whistling a guileless tune, Billy walked on, and had made it a full block before the braying began, and the kicking, and the call of outrage when someone burst out of the livery to investigate. Then Billy ran.

The mule, its lead rope snapping like a snake in the dusty street, clomped past him, braying with clownish teeth and swaying from back to front as if its spine were set at an angle; and behind this a pair of men coming on hard with murder in their eyes. Billy ducked through a loose board in a fence, crossed a weedy yard, then passed through his loop-hole in the adjacent fence. The clamor from the street was cacophonous, braying and shouting and shattering glass, probing the alleys and other byways, leaving Billy running full-out toward the eponymous spring, where he eyed the derelict chestnut and the possibility of a hiding place within its tangled roots.

It was cloyingly damp within the roots, with an aged smell of rot and soil and a cold draft that seemed to tickle up between his legs. He folded himself in deeper as the men searched this way and that in frustration before finally turning back. Billy exhaled in relief, and when he pushed his hand against a mossy rock to work his way out, his hand broke through into a void, scaring him beyond measure.

He wriggled around until he could see, and was surprised by a musty waft of cold air that grazed lazily at his cheeks. He found himself peering into a crumbling hole of moss and rot, and upon further expansion he could see that the ancient chestnut had rooted across an opening between rocks and that what he had found was actually a cave!

Caves were plentiful in the area, but all long sealed for safety. Billy had never explored one, but now he had the opportunity and he was intrigued. A little more excavating opened the entrance wide enough and he shimmied in, undeterred by the slimy wetness of the rocks. The angle of the entrance was quite shallow but trending downward. He followed this on elbows and knees until the light from the entrance became too dim to go on, but he had proceeded far enough by then, and the cave had widened enough, that he could stand and lift his fingertips to the damp and irregular ceiling.

Returning later with candles, he made a fuller exploration. Deep into the cave, above a conical pile of glazed rubble, water drizzled from the ceiling to splatter on the rubble, filtering through to feed a stream that ran off down a narrowing tunnel into stygian depths well beyond the small light of his candle.

Billy explored no farther. Fears of becoming wedged in a dank tunnel with frigid water flowing over his feet captured any courage he had of going on, and what he had already discovered was more than enough. There were bones lying about, disarticulated leavings, with some looking eerily human. The pioneer fathers had never found this cave, but the Indians obviously had. Their handiwork was all over, from bits of broken arrowheads to palms with spread fingers painted in outline on the drier walls.

Billy had always been intrigued by Indians, although most of what he knew came from a contraband western novel that he had rescued from a burning when he was six or so. The novel contained woodcuts of various Indian scenes, of conical tents called teepees, of bows and arrows and buffalo (an animal so much larger than the deer of the area that they seemed mythical), campfires and cradleboards and buckskins, and all in contravention to the narrative Preacher Prine opined of heathen savages destined for perdition. Billy got the sense that he would have preferred to be an Indian, and that he would have made a good one.

He would have war-whooped his way toward his twelfth birthday, but that was a sound printed words could not impart, and he had no model of it except a single line drawing in the book, so he would simply pat his mouth with his palm, utter a syncopated "whoop—whoop—whoop," and satisfy himself with that.

Six boys were sent away that year, two in the spring and four in the summer, leaving Billy, on his twelfth birthday, the oldest unmarried boy left standing around the pool. Preacher Prine's son Peter Prine, a gangly boy with droopy eyes and black, bowl-cut hair, was a few weeks younger than Billy. Preacher Prine also had a gaggle of dim-witted daughters who doubtless suffered from the early but (at least for Preacher Prine) fortuitous demise of their mother. The daughters had not been paired when they came of age, but instead served functionary roles in the church and elsewhere. They were Prine's vestal virgins, a term that meant nothing to Billy but did raise nettled eyebrows from the menfolk now and again.

Preacher Prine's pride was Peter, destined to carry on the license of his lineage through the lassitude of his flock. Billy despised the boy. Making Peter pay the price of his paternity was a problem that vexed Billy viscerally, but try as he might he simply could not manage the means to malign the boy under Prine's wary and watchful eye. Billy would have to await the day, but in the meantime a pair of urgencies intruded. The first was a disquieting sprouting of hairs in his nether regions, coupled with an abrupt and intense urge to see a girl naked.

Elle Trimble was Billy's age and, as Billy suddenly realized, very pretty, with golden locks, fair skin, and a sly smile that Billy had not yet learned to interpret; so he invited her to his cave, and she readily agreed, which caused him a period of palpitation but the course was set and so they went. He had dressed up his cave during the preceding two years, with burlap bags laid along the entrance to keep the slime off palms and knees, lanterns pirated from the livery, and kegs of elixir upended for seating and makeshift tables.

Elle crawled in behind Billy, heedless in her dark dress, then stood up in the cavern and marveled at the sight of pictographs quivering to life in the lantern light, and of jeweled stalactites like the spears of kings. She heard an omnipresent and not unpleasant tinkling of water, like a serenade of wind chimes catching gentle breezes. Billy's cave would have been wondrous if not for the presence of an almost overpowering odor.

"What is that smell?" she asked, a finger below her nose.

"It's bat droppings," Billy answered. "You get used to it. They say you can make gunpowder out of it, or something like that. I was thinking about making a cannon, maybe."

"Yuck." Elle eventually waved away the smell. "So what do you do in here?" she asked, edging away from awe and edging toward Billy, who could only step back in nervous chagrin.

"Nothin'," he said dumbly.

"So whaddaya wanna do now?" she asked with that smile he had yet to interpret, but which gave him a shiver nonetheless.

"Uh, I don't know."

"Well, you should think of something." She had her hands clasped in the small of her back now, and was perusing the art on the walls.

Billy came up beside her. "That's a buffalo, I think," he said, pointing toward one of the pictographs, whose colors were indeterminate through the overlapping shadows cast onto the walls. "They don't live around here anymore, I guess."

"I've read about them," she stated imperiously. "And Indians, too."

"You have?" Billy gaped. "How?"

"Do you remember John Hatchett?"

"Yeah, kind of."

"Well, he was my father's friend. When he came back he snuck some books in. Preacher Prine found them, and that's why...well, you know. Anyway, he gave some to me first and I hid them real good." She looked at Billy pointedly. "Not even you could find them."

Billy didn't take that as an insult or a challenge. He was instead mesmerized by her ears. "So what were they about?" he asked, his eyes never leaving her lobes.

Elle turned her lobes from his look, and with an inside smile pretended to resume her perusal. "They were about all kinds of things," she said offhandedly, as if engrossed in the ancient wall art. "Like outside there are cities so big that people have to live way up in the sky; and water comes out of pipes in your house and you don't have to boil it to make it hot; and there are machines you can drive without mules."

That sounded like fanciful talk to Billy, who guffawed at the very notion. "You're making that up," he said with certainty.

"I am not," she said just as certainly.

What a world that would be, he thought in wonder, but then he shivered at the idea of being banished to a place like that, a place that was wholly beyond his imagination, a place that would render him the inescapable imbecile in any group. "I don't know if I would like that," he said with less certainty than before.

"I would," Elle replied at once. "I would love to live in the sky and have hot water whenever I wanted it and not have to whip a smelly mule to get around."

"Uh..." Billy found that no further words would form, so he just loitered there and wondered what he should do next.

Elle waited, and wondered, and then snorted in consternation. "So do you wanna kiss me or what?"

"Huh?" Billy blanched. He wanted nothing more, but suddenly faced with it he felt as if he were a stammering six years old again. "I, uh..."

"Oh, please," and Elle leaned over and pecked him on the lips.

Billy blushed unseen in the wavering light, but at the same time felt a tingle that trickled all the way down to where the new hairs grew. The onus was now on him and he didn't know what to do with his hands, so he reached out a bit roughly for the softness that had lately begun to build beneath her bodice, and was disabused of that action with a slap across his face.

"What are you doing?" she demanded. "You're worse than Preacher Prine."

"Wha—what?" Billy rubbed his stinging cheek.

"You're hopeless, Billy Bailey." Elle spat this with mocking misery, and then she turned on her heel and fled the cave.

Billy sat bewildered, rubbing his cheek and wondering what went wrong.

Billy's second problem involved (as far as he knew) his impending banishment, and this required careful thinking, which went a long way toward banishing Elle from those same thoughts for the moment.

He sat in his cave, or in the tree behind his house, or sometimes on his bed well into the small hours puzzling the problem, yet no solution presented. Ideas turned in circles behind his eyes, which then overlapped other circles, and still others, forming a complicated spiral that became too difficult to hold in his head all at once. One idea returned over and over, though, the idea of making a cannon, to do what with he could not conceive, but there it was just the same.

He had never been exposed to adventurous stories of artillery, valor, and war, and yet a nebulous narrative still existed somehow, drawn as if from the ether to awe and inspire the youngsters, so Billy thought a cannon would be grand. The stern and burnished men at the smithy suspiciously offered little but bare hints, which led like breadcrumbs toward a possibility, but there the trail ended. The bat droppings, which they called guano (which sounded more like a gut disease) were a part of it, but what part remained unclear.

Books in general were nonexistent in Kingdom Spring, but there were still a few tomes of practical import lying about. Billy rummaged through these with frenetic energy as the year wore on, gleaning a fact here, incorporating it into another fact there, slowly but steadily building a puzzle of disparate and individually meaningless pieces. His latent studiousness impressed his surprised teacher, even drawing the notice of Preacher Prine, although Prine wasn't quite sure whether this portended well or ill.

Throughout, Elle was as aloof as a day-lit owl. Billy was grateful that she hadn't revealed the secret of his cave, but less than grateful when she would seem to refocus her attention on Peter whenever Billy was present. It was not so much a jealousy that tormented Billy, but the sore suffering of the rejected.

Winter came and went, the coldest in memory. Billy could barely breathe as the beauteous days of spring bore toward his banishment. An unfortunate fire in the apothecary shed provided an important puzzle piece. Flames like solid light leaped upward, blue-limned and with the heat to melt tin. It was a frantic affair putting out that fire, which resisted bucket after bucket of water with the stubbornness of a malingering mule. Billy crowded in with the rest to watch the desperate doings, the heat palpable even from afar, and then it came to him in a rush of imagination, and his head heated hotter than the leaping flames.

"Whoop—whoop—whoop," he hollered victoriously at the vexed villagers as he sprinted from the crush to his cave.

He returned in bare minutes with a small cloth bundle, took a circuitous path through various loopholes in order to get around back unseen, and then, airy and anxious with anticipation, hurled the bundle into the elixir-fed flames.

The explosion tore into the livery next door, scattering mules and saddle-sagging horses in a rush toward the crowd, the spectating villagers heaving aside as if by the sweep of a great hand. Billy lifted himself from the dirt and brushed at his knees and sooted cheeks. Elsewhere, Preacher Prine frowned. Wilson's Distilled Elixir, despicable as it was, still delivered a dependable dispensation to his pockets, but now it was gone, except for the few casks secreted in Billy's cave, of which even Elle entertained no present recollection; and as calamity careened through the streets of Kingdom Spring, for the first time Billy was not blamed.

Afterward, Billy set to work with clever determination. Had careful notice been given, he would have been seen stepping off the distance between the pool and his cave, his teacher would have been aware of the sums he surreptitiously scribbled, his mother would have recognized his glint of mischief, and Preacher Prine would have had premonitions of pending pandemonium.

Billy stood proudly at the pool on the appointed day, starched and steady and with a prominence that did not portend well for Prine and the people who pandered to him. Prine read from his bible in the gathering heat, Billy the sole remaining recipient of the dousing to come. Billy tapped a cramped toe in time, not with Preacher Prine's words but with the present Billy would soon provide, and he prayed it would come posthaste because the water in the pool was cold and Billy had no wish to be dipped into it.

Preacher Prine completed his reading, closed his bible and his eyes as he mouthed the customary prayer, and then it was time and he summoned Billy to his side. There was a shallow ledge beyond the lip of the pool. Prine stepped into the chill water and beckoned Billy forward, maintaining his stoic stamina despite his numbing feet—that is until Billy uttered a firm and convincing, "No."

Preacher Prine blinked twice in incomprehension while a murmur matriculated through the many gathered around.

"What did you say?" Preacher Prine summoned his indignation and followed on with, "You will step into these holiest of waters at once and be baptized."

"I will not," Billy barked back.

The red reached Prine's eyes then raced across his face, drawing a chuckle from Billy because this was a look similar to the one he had seen through the sunny window that day. People were beginning to edge back at this display of disregard for the august authority of the Prines.

"Why...why..." Prine sputtered. "The temerity of...I'll have you whipped, boy."

"No you won't," Billy said, holding fast and entirely too confident for Prine's comfort. Prine's face became redder yet, and the murmurs all around merged into moans of mortification.

With a gasp of righteous indignation, Preacher Prine took a first sopping step out of the pool, only to be rocked back by a muffled bellow from below. The ground shook as if the heavens had opened, loosing terror among the townsfolk and sending Preacher Prine off balance toward the frigid water. Faced with imminent immersion, Preacher Prine tossed his precious and indispensable bible onto dry ground, where Billy scooped it up quickly and stepped back from the tumult to come.

A sound like a distant but intense pop caught the attention of all, followed by a sluicing and slurping, and then, like a wicked wind, a whirlpool spun the chill waters of the pool, drawing Preacher Prine into the maw of the maelstrom and then down into the disastrous depths. Prine gave a final desperate cry as he was sucked with the last of the water into a funneled hole at the bottom of the pool; and then he was gone, the pool was empty, and Billy let loose a "Whoop—whoop—whoop" of triumph, which attracted the attention of none because all eyes were fixed on the horror the emptied pool now revealed.

Billy nudged between his numbed neighbors to see what held them so transfixed, and was taken aback himself at the sight of bones littered about the floor of the pool. There were hundreds of them, skulls and pelvises and leg bones and ribs, and then it was obvious and he wanted to be sick. The pioneer fathers had taken Kingdom Spring from the Indians, but those Indians hadn't been simply driven off, they had been massacred, their bodies tossed into a sinkhole, the serendipitous spring rerouted to fill the sinkhole and conceal the evidence; and here, for generations, the villagers had been baptized, not in the holiest of water but in undeniable death.

The same wrenching realization raced through them all. The vestal virgins wretched. Sturdy men went white. Peter had Elle by the hand and was backing away with a hounded look in his hound-dog eyes. Billy glanced up to see Peter and Elle edging away, and snapped out in a voice that had become noticeably deeper of late, "Take them!"

Men who would have formerly consigned him to a foreign life beyond Kingdom Spring jumped to his order and seized the two, who struggled futilely at their turn of fortune. The villagers had quieted, all eyes on Billy, who thumbed through Prine's bible and nodded grimly at the annotations. He laughed when he read that Peter was to be paired with Elle, and that he himself was to be matched with a loathsome girl named Lucy. So he wasn't to have been banished after all, although being forced to live with Lucy would have made him lament that.

Billy probed the possibilities, then smiled as cunningly as a cougar. He swept the girls with his gaze, discounting Elle because there were even fairer girls in the group, not to mention a variety of vestal virgins to vanquish.

"Banish them!" he shouted toward Peter and Elle.

"Who put you in charge?" Elle's father shouted back.

"I did," Billy countered with conviction.

"We'll see about that," Elle's father spat indignantly as he lurched to take Billy in hand.

The women, led by Adine, moved then, gathering around Billy and as fierce in the eyes as Amazons, for they alone knew that Billy was their only future, a future they were compelled to protect come what may. The men quailed before their quixotic women, inured to the inevitability of impending indignity.

Thirteen-year-old Billy Bailey took position in Preacher Prine's place at the head of the now-emptied pool, the bible firmly in his hands and with a devious grin on his face.

THE SUMMER OF SERENDIPITY

The little girls came single file down the shallow creek, picking their way barefoot around overhanging thickets and through algae-clotted water to reach his section of the creek, the only part deep enough after a good rain to form a pool the little girls could splash in on a wilting summer afternoon.

Nelson O'Donnell sat in the rocker on his high porch and followed the girls' progress as if they were advancing enemy scouts and he a secreted spy. He'd rather they not come on his property, but kids were so combatively recalcitrant these days that it was better to let them alone than to go down there and try to run them off. There would probably be some reprisal in that, some petty vandalism that would be even worse than the noisy gaggle he was forced to endure most afternoons. They'd grow up by and by, meld into whatever stunted lives lay ahead of them, and then peace and quiet would return once more. He could only hold out hope.

Nelson was a man who simply did not like people. People were messy. People were fickle. They were deceitful and disingenuous, palsied with all manner of troubles and turbulence that they were more than willing—with scant if any sense of propriety or decorum—to splash on others with less restraint than those little girls splashing in the creek. Nelson found people to be tedious, tiring, and wantonly undignified. He was of the belief that if you allowed most people the opportunity of self-indulgence, they would exercise that opportunity to its extremes no matter how imposing or obnoxious they became. In order to live peacefully, therefore, it was prudent to avoid people as much as possible.

He had never married. He had no children. He had taken early retirement from the phone company at the age of fifty-five, where he'd spent far too many years grubbing money from surly customers who refused to pay their bills by mail and who heaped abuse on him for every misadventure they'd ever had with their service. The day he'd walked out, amid little fanfare, was perhaps the happiest day of his life. He lived now in blessed solitude in an old family farmhouse on what remained of the family estate. A brother and sister had carved out swathes of the estate years ago and had then sold them off, inviting trailer-park strangers into his once-placid environment. Nelson thought as little of his siblings as he did of people in general.

The little girls were a case in point. They lived on a hillside farther up the creek, in a dilapidated double-wide behind a screen of rambling bushes that kept it all hidden except during the deepest of winter. Nelson had played up there when he was a child, when the creek had flowed through a stand of tall woods aflutter with redbirds, when fish could be caught in the wetter seasons, and where green turtles had plopped as he passed near. Those woods were long gone, now just brush and awful litter and a mildewed double-wide that was sagging in the center.

It was a blessing that he couldn't see the place from his porch. He could hear them, though, the little girls giggling and shrieking at whatever mischief they were making, often a woman's scolding voice, sometimes the scolding voice of a man, sometimes a heated argument in the night, the constant back and forth of a ratty truck with a blown muffler, once the crack of a gunshot. He wondered why the sheriffs stayed away. Seen from the highway up there, the place was a pack rat's nest, a plot of accumulated spoor strewn about with less reverence than a city dump in a hard wind. He sighed at the thought and was thankful again for the wild bushes, otherwise that sty would be his view over breakfast every morning.

Otherwise it was pleasant on the porch, where the shade of big oaks tempered a searing southerly wind. Beyond the broad canopies of the oaks, the sun shone remorselessly on limpid grass and listless shrubs. Even the birds were quiet, waiting out the suffocating afternoon heat in their cool knothole niches. A lone kestrel studied him from a power line across the way, its lively colors blanched in the shimmering air. There was a time, he thought with a stab of melancholy, when he could work hard in heat like this and shrug it off. Lately—and in truth for some years now—the heat sapped his energy too quickly for him to venture even the smallest chore out in the brunt of it, so he spent more and more of his afternoons sheltered on the porch, with his newspaper in hand and a cool glass of iced tea close by.

Shaking the fold out of his newspaper, he continued to peruse its columns. There was not much good in the world, he noted with despair, but when had there ever been? Wars were always being fought, children were always starving somewhere, and the prices for farm goods were always falling. There were always too many people, who over-bred their despoiled countries and then picked up en masse to migrate elsewhere and repeat the process. Excepting advances in technology, he could just as well have been reading a newspaper from decades past.

The little girls were at the pool now, splashing and carrying on as if the heat were no hindrance whatsoever but instead an excuse to get out and make noise. The water was barely deep enough to cover their ankles, and yet they carried on as if they were shoulder-deep in a lake. One pudgy little girl was sitting in it and flapping her arms as if she were coming up for air, while another girl lay flat on her stomach in the turbid water and kicked her feet. Two older girls of about the same age sat on the muddy bank and blew dandelion seeds into the stagnant air. The seeds settled like snow in the hair of two other girls, who shrieked in complaint but with grins on their faces. The girls were raucous and loud, and had finally found Nelson's limit.

He folded his newspaper and tossed it aside in aggravation, then stared over at the girls while trying to think what he should or could do. After some time spent considering every outcome he could imagine, and what he would say in each instance, he took his cane in hand, tottered down the steps, and made his way across his dry, crunching yard toward the creek.

The girls went taut as he approached, frozen in whatever they'd been doing when they had first caught sight of him. The pudgy girl squirted a stream of water from her mouth, as if she had been holding her cheeks full but could hold them no longer. The girl on her stomach peered at him with neither frown nor smile but instead with a quizzical look, as if he were something new to discover. The two girls on the bank held empty dandelion stems, pursed lips locked in mid blow, while the seeds settled unmolested on the heads of the remaining two girls.

"Hello girls," he announced himself uncomfortably. He didn't want to frown and scare them, nor did he want to smile and encourage them. Instead he went for a bland expression, hoping to split the difference.

The little girl lying on her stomach sat up and gave him a tentative wave with a willowy hand. "Hi," she said.

"I, uh, I saw you all playing..."

No comment came, just six pairs of fixed eyes that possessed equal amounts of apprehension and expectation.

"I, uh, I used to play in this creek when I was a boy," he went on with a dry swallow. It was best to find some common ground, he'd decided, something unthreatening that would divert them from coming back at him with mischief. "Are you all, uh, having fun?"

"Yeah," the little girl who had waved said. She smiled now, revealing teeth that resembled uneven piano keys. The rest of the girls still held statued poses.

"Uh, huh..." he nodded. Despite his mental rehearsal, he had no idea what to say next. "I, uh...when I was a boy I used to catch frogs and turtles in this creek."

The pudgy girl looked around sharply, not in alarm but in sudden revelation. "Really?" she said.

"Uh, huh. I used to catch them all the time."

"Where are they?" the pudgy girl asked with a shrug.

"Oh, under rocks and things."

All the girls gazed up and down the creek now, as if seeing it with new eyes. The bedrock was limestone, the creek was ancient, and rocks large and small and in their dozens crowded the banks, protruding from mud and tufts of grass. Some of the rocks were sharp, some were worn by eons of running water, and some glittered with minerals. Between them here and there were shiny bits of metal and glass, the detritus of generations past.

"Can we look for frogs and turtles, too?" the girl who had waved asked.

"Sure, if you want to."

"Awesome!"

She jumped up, went to a large rock, and began trying to haul it out of the bank. She was a lithe little girl, dressed in a thin shift that fell only as far as her knees and now clung to her wet skin almost transparently. Nelson quickly averted his eyes, leaned back on his cane and up at the sun. The girls were all up now, helping tug at the rock. It finally came out with a plomp and a splash.

"There's nothing there," one of the girls said.

"You just have to keep looking," Nelson said, squinting at the glare.

"Okay."

And what ensued was industry, curiosity, and above all, quiet. Nelson smiled at his success and returned to his porch.

The summer days proceeded lazily and hazily, sometimes not even a stir of air to rustle the leaves. Nelson marked each day on his porch with his sweating glass of iced tea and a newspaper that continued to seem no different from the day before. And yet he was content with his quiet life, made quieter still as the girls explored in earnest up and down the creek bank, the reward of some creek creature always awaiting the next rock they levered aside, although up until now their quest had been fruitless. It was much too hot, Nelson knew. Any aquatic creatures would have burrowed down into the cooling mud, or else would have migrated farther downstream where the water was deeper. The girls didn't know that, though.

Over the top of his newspaper, he observed their futile quest each day. Their energy was astounding, their focus fixed on a discovery that would validate their efforts regardless how much work they put into it. He would have been like that as a child, too. Did an old man once sit on a porch and watch him as he had explored the creek? Perhaps so, perhaps not. What did it matter, anyway?

Days passed.

He had been driven inside on one day, when even in the shade of the porch the heat had become unbearable. He sat in his easy chair with his tea and his newspaper, and eventually dozed late into the dusky afternoon. He awoke with a start as his doorbell chimed, a sound so rare that it took him a moment to place it. He got up unsteadily and went to a front door that was seldom used, the doorbell chiming again with an implied urgency that made him growl at the impudence of it. He yanked the door open, fully girded to upbraid that impudence, but then wiped that expression quickly away when he found one of the little girls there, the one who had waved at him, grinning widely and holding out a warty black toad that was practically the size of a kitten.

"Look what I found!" the girl gushed breathlessly, her piano teeth exposed to the gums and her eyes lit with excitement. Her legs were muddy from boney knees to bare feet. Her hands and arms were streaked with it as well, and there was a smear of it on her cheek. Her dress was just as filthy, and Nelson briefly worried that this girl's mother might blame him for the mess.

The rest of the girls caught up and gathered around, scrambling up the steps to his front door, all wearing skinned knees and infectious grins. They were pressing in unabashedly close, as if all boundaries had been abolished by the thinnest thread of familiarity from their first meeting. By temperament he normally would have snapped them back with a sharp word or two, but he couldn't bring himself to drive those grins from their faces.

"Well, now," Nelson found himself smiling instead, "look what you've got there."

"Serendipity caught him all by herself," the pudgy little girl, who had the flaming hair and blue eyes of a Viking, said. "He was in a hole and she stuck her hand all the way in."

"You did, did you?" Nelson was unsure how to moderate his voice. Speaking to children took a skill he'd never indulged. "So is that your name? Serendipity?" he asked, and his tone must have been all right because the girl with the toad nodded eagerly. She was a pretty girl despite her awkward teeth. She had fine, fair hair, intelligent, soft brown eyes, and a delicate face. "Well then, Serendipity, what are you going to do with him now?"

A puzzled frown formed around teeth that still poked through. "I don't know."

"Well," Nelson said, "maybe you can play with him for a little while—careful so you don't hurt him—then you should let him go and maybe you can catch him again sometime."

"Yeah," one of the bigger girls exclaimed. "Let's ketch 'em again!"

And then as one the mob banged down the steps, all elbows and knees, and raced back to the creek. Nelson watched them go, an unfamiliar smile still in place. "She stuck her hand in a hole," he mused while shaking his head. "She's a fearless little thing."

His doorbell chimed again the next day, although this time it wasn't the girls. The expectant smile he had put on fell when he opened the door to find his lawn man standing there huffing in the heat, hands on hips and wearing a sullen scowl. Surely the man must shave sometimes, was Nelson's first thought. The sweat-beaded shadow on the man's jaws looked like oily, coarse-grained emery paper.

"Mr. Nelson," the man announced sharply if not also accusingly. Nelson grimaced. Try as he had, and with increasing levels of opprobrium, he had never been able to disabuse this man of addressing him with such unprofessional familiarity.

"I prefer Mister *O'Donnell*," Nelson said with thinly veiled derision.

The man glowered suspiciously for a moment, then dismissed that comment and continued: "Mr. Nelson, those kids are throwin' rocks up in the yard. I hit one with the mower and broke a damn blade."

Nelson winced, not at the man's mishap but at the man's blithe refusal to offer the proper address even after having been corrected. "I'm sorry about that. Perhaps you should look more carefully next time."

"There ain't gonna be a next time if you don't make 'em stop."

"They're not my kids. You should say something to them."

"Well, they're not my kids either. It's not my yard and it's not my problem. You gotta do somethin' about it or else I ain't gonna come here no more."

With that the man huffed and took off, and Nelson was glad to see him go. Nelson despised that uncouth man, but there was no one else around to do the mowing and Nelson had gotten too old to do it himself. He sighed at this latest disturbance of his peace. He had no choice but to go down and talk to the girls, which would extend his exposure to them that little bit more.

He reached back for his cane, then went down the steps and across the yard. Serendipity saw him coming and gave him a friendly wave and a toothy smile. Before he'd completed another step, the whole gaggle was running excitedly toward him. He groaned and stood still, leaning on his cane.

"Look what I found! Look what I found!" The pudgy girl bounced up the bank with something in her hand, which soon proved to be an old baby food jar filled with murky water. "I caught him right down there." She thrust a finger out behind her and in the general direction of the creek. There was a minnow in the jar, just beginning to turn belly-up in its last throes.

"Well, now..." Nelson had steeled himself for a proper scolding, but those feelings withered in the cheeky, ebullient face that demanded his full attention in lieu of the others. The little girl dipped and tipped and jostled with the others in order to hold his eye, as if no one had ever paid the least attention to her before and this was finally her chance. Nelson sensed this, although he wouldn't have been able to put it into words, so he gave her his attention, even bending a creaking knee for a better look. "...it looks as if you caught yourself a minnow."

"Yeah, it's a minnow." She edged even closer to him, the same way a dog seeking affection will huddle against a person's leg. She frowned. "But I think he's gonna die."

"He probably will," Nelson said, checking a hand that had reached out instinctively to pat the girl consolingly on the head. "It's too hot for minnows, and the water has too much algae in it. It's not anything you did," he added in case she was feeling guilty.

"Oh, okay," she said, if not relieved then at least not despondent.

"So girls," he said hesitantly. They were all focused on him intently and still breathing the excitement of the pudgy girl's find. Nelson wasn't sure what to say. He had diverted them with this activity and that had gone well enough, but he could anticipate the rebellious resentment that would follow what he had to say next, resentment that might lead to the very mischief he had feared, or else, and perhaps worse, it might lead to disappointment. He didn't want to see disappointment in their eyes, and couldn't tell himself why it mattered to him at all.

"So girls," he pushed himself creakily erect. "You've been throwing rocks up in the yard." A few frowns formed, and he searched quickly for something to ameliorate that. "Uh, I don't mind if you do that but the lawn man hit one with his mower and he's a little mad."

"You're not mad, are you?" Serendipity asked with a worried look that weighed on his heart.

"No, no, of course not, but maybe you could throw them back in the creek when you're finished?"

He stiffened himself for the rush of objections and indignation they were certainly about to heap on him, but instead one of the older girls said, as lightly as if it were the most obvious thing, "Yeah, we should do that. C'mon y'all, let's do it right now!"

The girls scattered as if on an Easter egg hunt, probing the grass and low spots for rocks and then tossing them into the creek with splashes that came like hail, muddy gingham dresses clinging to muddy knees, their smudged faces smiling and happy. Nelson turned back toward the house, feeling peculiarly light in his steps. These girls weren't like the other children he'd encountered in his life, those petulant brats who whined and cried and grabbed at everything and were never satisfied with anything, abetted by parents whose behavior, in its older manifestation, was just as horrendous. These girls could make easy play out of a hellishly hot day, and there was something invigorating about that.

He went out the next morning before the heat came up and before the girls roused toward their riparian explorations. It was the kind of steamy morning that always fogged his eyeglasses. Dew clung to grass that would be desiccated again by noon. Jays cawed their morning calls from treetop to treetop, while wispy eastern clouds reflected the first clean yellow shades of the coming day.

His steps left wet footprints in the revived grass as he made his way down to the creek to check on the girls' work from yesterday. He found, to his unexpected delight, that not only had all the rocks in his yard been removed, but that the girls had used them to build a dam around the pool, creating a deeper basin where silvery minnows darted about as if their world were infinite. It was ingenious and imaginative work to have come from such young girls, which stirred him with an odd sense of pride.

Back inside and with the breakfast dishes washed and put away, he had a thought that the girls deserved some kind of reward for their hard work and ingenuity. This was a puzzling thought not only because he couldn't explain to himself why he cared at all, but also because, even so, he had no idea what little girls liked. Dolls, he suspected, but there were certainly none of those in his musty old house. But then, were these rambunctious girls really the kind who played with dolls?

He thought on this long as he rummaged through drawers and old steamer trunks, revisiting mementos from ages past, mementos that too often rekindled a youth lost so long ago that those memories seemed to belong to someone else. It was during his search through a steamer trunk in his boyhood bedroom upstairs that he came across his rock collection from those early years. Each rock had been polished to a glossy luster by a machine that used to run in the dime store in town, a store that was it-self now a relic of memory. He held a glistening rock in his knobby hand and remembered the feel of it exactly, the soft texture of the smooth surface, so at odds with nature and yet so prettily swirled with color and reflected light. He had sat for hours as a child studying these rocks and the colorful constellations they contained. They would make the perfect gift, he decided right then, so he picked out six of the larger ones and dropped them into his pocket, paused a moment then added one more.

The girls weren't apprehensive when he came out this time, instead they smiled and waved him closer to admire their handiwork.

"Look what we made," Serendipity beckoned with an innocent en-thusiasm that was almost heartbreaking.

"Well, I see," he said, beaming unconsciously and pretending to be seeing their construction for the first time. "You've built yourselves a fish weir. That's very smart, girls."

"It was my idea," the pudgy girl hollered as she bounded up the bank to claim the center of his attention.

"Yeah, it was Anthem's idea," Serendipity seconded from down in the creek, where she stood up to her thin calves in their newly deep-ened pool.

"So your name's Anthem?" Nelson asked the redheaded little girl, who was bouncing from foot to foot to keep his eyes looking her way.

"Uh, huh," she said.

"What's a weir?" one of the other girls asked.

"A weir is an enclosure for catching fish, and I bet you've caught a lot of them."

"We have, we have!" Anthem repeated, tugging at his hand as she did so.

"Well, Anthem," Nelson bent his reluctant knee as far as it would go, finally all the way to the ground and now he was on level with the little girl's insistent sapphire gaze. "That was very smart. I know you all will have a lot of fun now."

"Yeah," she said. "It's fun."

With a grimace and a hard grip on his cane, Nelson pushed himself back up. "I was looking through an old box and I found something I think you girls might like."

"What?"

"What?"

The girls were suddenly around him in a pack, Anthem with a possessive arm around his knee, and he couldn't help but smile. He reached into his pocket and took out the rocks. "I found these."

"Whoa!"

"Wow!"

"Pretty!"

Anthem made a grab for the rocks but he pulled his hand away. "Now hold on, Anthem. It just so happened that I had six of them, and, well, there are six of you, so it has to be fair. Which of you is the oldest?"

"We are," the two older girls said excitedly and in unison, waving their hands above the others.

"Hmm," Nelson said, perplexed.

"I'm Millie," one girl said.

"I'm Minnie," said the other.

"We're twins," they said together.

"And we're twelve," Millie appended.

"Hmm," Nelson said again. Both girls had stringy hair that might wash out to near blond, but the resemblance beyond that was hard to discern with their smudged faces and mismatched dresses. They were the same height, almost exactly so, and their feet looked the same, four sets of toes plugged with mud. "Okay," Nelson decided, "Millie and Minnie get to go first."

The twins pushed forward and studied the rocks in his palm as if this were the most important decision they would ever make. "Hurry up," Anthem chided them, tugging at Nelson's knee now and trying to get him to look down.

"Okay, I'll take this one," Millie said.

"And I'll take this one," Minnie followed.

"Ooh, pretty," Serendipity beamed.

"Okay, who's next?" Nelson asked.

A curiously dark-haired girl shyly raised her hand. "I'm Aliana," she said demurely. "I'm eleven."

"Okay, Aliana. Come and choose the one you like the best."

Aliana was not like the other girls. It was not only her dark hair and closed expression but also the way she approached slowly, as if wary of what might happen. Aliana didn't scrutinize the rocks for long, but rather seemed to take the first one her fingers found. Then she retreated to the periphery, rolling and poking the rock in her palm.

"And now..." Nelson began.

"Me! Me!" Serendipity shrieked, wildly waving her hand. "I'm ten."

"So you're ten, are you Serendipity?" She nodded quickly and eagerly. "Okay, then it's your turn."

Serendipity surveyed the dwindling supply of rocks, and then chose one that was not the biggest by far. "I like this one," she said. "It's pretty."

"Yes it is," Nelson agreed, which drew Serendipity's keyboard smile.

There were two girls left. Nelson's eyes went from Anthem to the other, a girl whose hair was similar to Serendipity's, and who had the same eager brown eyes, but who seemed more frail than the rest. "I'm next," the girl said. "I'm Shine and I'm nine." She smiled.

"That's a good rhyme, Shine," he said, and she smiled even wider. "So which one do you like the most?"

"I like this one." She made up her mind right then and took a rock.

"But there's only one for me," Anthem pouted. "I don't get to choose and that's not fair."

"Hmm, you're right. That's not fair at all. Wait, what's this I have in my other pocket?" He reached into his other pocket and brought out another rock as if by magic. "Well what a surprise," he said. "There just happened to be another one in my pocket that I didn't know about, so now there's two and you get to choose."

Anthem was now beaming and bouncing like a puppy, and standing taller, too. "I'm, Anthem and I'm eight," she announced forthrightly, and then she reached out and chose a rock of her own.

"Okay, girls," Nelson said then, growing weary in the heat. "It's getting too hot for me so I'd better go in now."

"Aw."

"Aw."

"It's okay. I'll see you all later."

Nelson made it back to his porch with effort, where he dropped into his rocker and fanned his face. The girls were all sitting along the creek bank quietly studying their rocks, as if each held a universe all its own.

Even that little bit of excitement had whittled him down, so he soon went inside for a nap, and was awoken by the chime of his doorbell in what seemed like minutes—but was actually hours—later. He trudged to the door, rubbing his eyes, and opened it on the girls, who were huddled tightly around Anthem, who was proudly holding up a box turtle.

"I caught 'em!" she exclaimed, tipping and bouncing as always.

"My, my," Nelson smiled sleepily, "isn't that a fine looking turtle?"

"Yeah, I'm gonna play with him and let him go so we can ketch him again."

"That's a really good idea, hun," he said. He looked off to the west, where the sun was settling into pink and lavender layers above distant hills. "It's a little late, isn't it? Shouldn't you girls be home eating dinner about now?"

"Naw, it's okay," Serendipity spoke up. "My mama told us to go and play in the creek until she said so."

Something about that set off a disturbed pang, but the girls seemed as cherubic as ever, just in need of baths and clean dresses. "Okay, well then..." He couldn't think what else to add. "Uh, you all be careful then, okay?"

"Okay, mister," and they spun off to race back to the creek. Serendipity paused mid-step and turned back. "Hey, mister?" she asked toothily and with her smile still firmly in place. "What's your name, anyway?"

"I'm Mister O'Donnell," he answered.

"Okay, Mister O'Donnell. See ya," and then she ran off to join the rest.

From then on his doorbell would chime regularly, usually as he was napping and as the sun was descending into the weather of the day. He had been moved by the girls, he could admit that to himself, but their visits were becoming an annoyance. Sometimes they brought the creatures they'd caught, frogs and toads, the turtle once again, minnows, and on one particularly exciting occasion, a crawdad. Often, though, they would come empty-handed, lounge on the steps and smile hello, and he would smile in return no matter how grumpy he felt.

On one of these visits, Serendipity commented, "Your house is pretty, Mister O'Donnell."

"Why thank you, Serendipity."

"Can we go inside and see?"

There was no telling what kind of chaos that would invite, what new accommodation would be generated to intrude upon his peace. Still, Nelson would have let them come in anyway, it was just that the world wasn't as idyllic as the creek bank. The girls needed to understand that.

"Serendipity," he said gently. "You should never go into a stranger's house unless your parents are with you."

"Why not?"

"Well, uh, because you don't know what might happen."

"What might happen?"

She wore the blank expression of profound puzzlement, they all did, as if the world beyond their happy hollow had never reached in with its ugly touch; and no matter what, he could never be that heartrendingly frank with these girls. That was a lesson that needed to come from their parents, not him.

"Your parents might get mad," he deflected instead.

"Mama won't get mad," Serendipity said as if the very idea were ludicrous. "And you're not a stranger."

Nelson sighed but with a warm smile. "Your mother hasn't met me, Serendipity, so to her I'm a stranger. If she comes with you, I'll let you see the house."

That seemed to satisfy the girls for the moment, and Nelson blew a breath of relief.

As the days marched into August, the girls' mother never showed herself beyond the hollering he could often hear through the bushes. He continued to watch the girls from his porch in the early afternoons. They were always busy, always moving, always bending and probing and then shooting upright with something cupped in their hands that the others would then rush to see. Periodically they would spare a look his way and then wave exuberantly, as if they hadn't seen him in weeks. Serendipity never failed to wave, never failed to smile, even on the grayest days when the weather threatened. Each little girl was unique, each incredibly happy in defiance of their circumstances, and each irreproachably polite, but it was Serendipity he was most pleased to see each day. There was something about the girl, some undefinable difference from the others. He kept a snapshot of her in his mind.

One hazy afternoon, as waves of goldenrod dipped their yellow feather-duster flowers toward the open sun of the creek, the girls came in their usual procession. Rather than continuing down the creek, though, they turned into his backyard and approached him on his porch, walking with the tentative steps of a fawn nosing out something new. Anthem was at their head, a mason jar stuffed with goldenrod flowers in her hands and a curious smile on her face.

"We brought you some flowers," she said, craning to see him on his high porch.

Nelson was so surprised that he sputtered before he could speak. "Well, uh...uh. Well, that's very nice of you. You can bring them up to me. It's okay if you come on the porch."

Each girl seemed to jump with joy, wide grins replacing hesitant smiles. They thumped noisily up the back steps then around the corner to where he sat, each girl breaking off to explore a different part of this new world. Anthem proffered the flowers with a smile that had gone shy.

"Why, thank you, Anthem. They're very pretty."

She tipped up and down on bare toes. "Do you like 'em?"

"I do. I do very much." She continued to tip up and down, hands clasped behind her back and eyes going everywhere but on him for a change. Nelson smiled knowingly. "You can go look around if you want."

"Yea!" she squealed, and then she romped off.

The porch wrapped all the way around the house, offering high views toward hills and hollows and the neighboring farms, a view the girls had never witnessed from the track of their world until then. It was a new universe to explore, new things to see, new dreams to form.

"There's a man on a tractor way over there!" Millie and Minnie announced excitedly.

"Haven't you seen a tractor before?" Nelson asked them, incredulous because they all lived in farm country after all.

"Yeah." Millie's smile went flat. "But not from our house. We can't see anything from there."

"We can hear you though," Minnie said. "Well, sometimes."

"Sometimes I can hear you, too," Nelson said with a laugh. Bumping and thumping was going on all around the house, but there was nothing the girls could get into that would hurt anything, only hanging plants and bird feeders, a few wind chimes, and a pair of rockers on the other side.

Millie and Minnie ran off, and then with heavy, padded thumps, Serendipity came around the corner with one of those rockers. She could barely lift the thing, and had to pause every few steps to set it down.

"Can I sit here?" she asked.

At first aggravated that she'd moved his rocker, he quickly shrugged that off. He hadn't used that rocker in years, and hadn't sat on that side of the house since he couldn't remember when, fully exposed as it was to the afternoon sun, and too cold in the spring and fall.

"Sure you can," he said, and to his surprise she pushed and tugged it right up next to him. Sweat bees had already found Anthem's goldenrods, which he had placed on his side table. One of the bees had taken a plunge into his tea. He dipped it out with a finger, flicked it away, and took a sip. "So," he asked Serendipity then, "how do you like the view?"

"It's pretty here," she said sweetly.

"Yes, it is pretty," he nodded, followed by silence as he had no idea how to hold a conversation with a child. Serendipity was practically swallowed by the big rocker. She bumped her feet and rocked strenuously, but always with a smile that sometimes seemed to go far off. "So," he said after a moment. There was a question he'd never asked them but which prodded at him constantly. "Are all of you girls—are you sisters?"

"Yeah, kinda," she answered, distracted by a clutch of goldfinches chattering at a feeder. "They're yellow!" she exclaimed, pointing at the birds. "They're so pretty."

"They're goldfinches," Nelson informed her. "The males are bright yellow in the summer when they're breeding."

"What does that mean, breeding?"

Nelson took an uncomfortable breath. "Uh, it's when the males help the females make eggs."

"They *do* that?" she asked, turning to him as if she thought he'd gone crazy.

"Yes, they do," he chuckled, warming around the collar.

"Hmm."

"So, you say all these girls are your sisters?"

"Yeah, kinda," and now she was looking off again. "Shine and me have the same mom, and Aliana and Anthem have the same mom, and Millie and Minnie have the same mom, and Shine and Anthem and me have the same dad, and Millie and Minnie and Aliana have the same dad."

Nelson's brows rose as he tried to put that in order. Serendipity seemed as unperturbed as the creek was by rain.

"Well," Nelson cleared his throat, "you have a big family, then."

"Yeah, it's pretty big."

The rest of the girls came bounding around the corner just then, plopping down around the two rockers and idling in the shade. Anthem followed a caterpillar's progress, pushing it along with a finger. The girls were bored now, and Nelson felt that the responsibility had fallen on him to do something about it.

"Do you girls like candy?" he ventured.

"Yeah!"

"Yeah!"

All eyes were bright with anticipation.

"Okay. You all hold on and I'll see what I can find."

He had a tin of chocolates that had come at Christmas. Sugar made his teeth ache, so when sweets came they sat on the countertop until they were old enough to throw out. He carried the tin out to the girls, who looked on with anxious astonishment. "Just a couple for each of you," he admonished them gently. "If it ruins your dinner your parents will be upset with me."

"Thanks, Mister O'Donnell!"

The girls crowded in like kittens to a milk bowl, but each took only two pieces and he was surprised by their restraint.

"Okay, girls," he announced then. "It's time for my nap. You can play on the porch for as long as you want."

"Okay."

"Thanks, Mister O'Donnell."

He left the girls there, giggling and licking their fingers, and when he lay down for his nap he could hear them playing beyond his window and he didn't mind.

The creek had dried up in the late summer drought, just bleached stone now, the stinking husks of dead algae, and the occasional desiccated minnow flattened into the stone as if it were an emerging fossil. The girls spent their days on the porch, increasingly bored but Nelson couldn't come up with anything more to keep them entertained. He'd brought out picture books, playing cards, and a rickety croquet set that he'd used as a child in this very yard. The girls had taken to each new activity with enthusiasm, an enthusiasm that waned as the days went by. He wondered—not for the first time—why these girls didn't go home to play.

The girls never complained—that wasn't it—only that their smiles were less lively on these sweltering days, and that was in its way heart wrenching. Serendipity always went for the rocker when the girls came, the rest of the girls ceding it to her as if by some innate understanding. Nelson didn't mind sitting with Serendipity. She never pressed him for something to do or for something to say, and always chirped something pleasant when he first encountered her each day.

Soon his routine was not much different than it had ever been, news-paper, iced tea, birds and shade and sometimes a cooling breeze, along with a quiet that seemed as if it no longer fit properly. The girls would be all around him, gangly and sun-browned and deep in their own thoughts. The days passed.

As August slid into September, Nelson asked the girls if they shouldn't be in school.

"We're homeschooled now," Serendipity said without emphasis.

"Yeah," Anthem jumped up. "Serendipity made an A but the teacher gave her an F."

"They don't like us there," Aliana muttered shyly.

"And Mama got mad," Shine added.

Overcome with a sudden permeating sadness, Nelson held his tongue. Serendipity was smart, he could tell that about her. She should be in a school where she could show them all how smart she really was. It wasn't his place to say anything, though. It wasn't his place.

Days later, the girls didn't come. There'd been some kind of commo-tion over at their property, but Nelson couldn't make out what. Another day with no girls, and Nelson began to worry. Then he heard Anthem's high-pitched cackle from beyond the bushes, as well as Millie and Min-nie's deeper voices at play, so he knew, with relief, that everything must be all right over there, or at least as right as it could be. Why the girls didn't come was not his business. Perhaps their mother was teaching them now. Homeschooling would have to be a time-consuming endeav-or, probably occupying most of their days.

He was surprised, then, to come out one morning to find Serendipity in the rocker. The sun was up but it was still early, still quiet beyond the bushes. He had come to look forward to the cacophony of voices beyond those bushes. If the girls couldn't be here, at least he knew they were there. He could identify each of their voices, imagine each girl at play as if he were there watching them: Anthem bouncing, shy Aliana, Shine singing a rhyming song, Serendipity finding something new in everything she saw, Millie and Minnie riding herd as the eldest. Their voices serenaded him each day over his newspaper, leaked through his window as he lay for his nap. He felt they were his girls, and that was odd but that's the way he felt.

Serendipity smiled as he approached, the way she always did, as if nothing in the world could bring her low.

"Hi, Mister O'Donnell," she waved.

"Hello, Serendipity." He was smiling himself, and with something more than his usual greeting. "I haven't seen you in a while."

"Yeah, Mama made us stay home."

"Huh. Where are the rest of the girls?"

She shrugged. "Reading, I guess."

"Does your mother know you're here by yourself?"

She shrugged again. "I don't know."

As he tottered closer, his heart dropped and water came into his eyes. Serendipity's delicate face was badly bruised, turning an ugly yellow on her left cheek and up around her eye. Her hair hid much of it. Nelson staggered.

"Serendipity, what happened?"

She was smiling still, as if nothing were out of the ordinary, but she knew what he meant.

"It's nothin'," she shrugged insouciantly. "Mama's boyfriend gets mad sometimes is all."

"Your mama's *boyfriend*?" he muttered, shock settling in and chilling his blood.

"Yeah, it doesn't hurt or anything. Oh," she was suddenly animated, "I saw a goldfinch! They're so pretty. I like them the most, but those other ones, the red ones?"

"Cardinals," he said numbly.

"Yeah, cardinals. They're pretty, too."

Nelson wiped his eyes and sat heavily, forcing a smile onto lips that wanted to twist in rage. "I have a book with pictures of birds," he said with effort. "Would you like to see it?"

"Yeah!" she exclaimed with all of her usual enthusiasm.

"Okay, I'll be right back."

They sat together for an hour, flipping pages, Serendipity so close that he could have wrapped a protective arm around her. He read to her about birds, identified them in the photos and pointed out the actual birds in his yard. By the time they heard Serendipity's mother call from beyond the bushes, Serendipity had slid so close to him that she was all but in his lap. She was safe, and he felt safe, but now she had to go.

"That's Mama callin', Mister O'Donnell, so I gotta go."

"Okay," he said sadly.

He watched her skit across the yard, looking over her shoulder every few steps to beam her implacable smile, and then she crossed the creek and plunged into the bushes for what Nelson somehow knew, with trembling lips and welling eyes, would be the last time.

He sat at his breakfast table staring at his old-fashioned rotary phone and warred with himself. He should go over there, he convinced himself in one thought. He should wade through the garbage and bang on that mildewed vinyl door and demand that Serendipity—that all the girls—should come stay with him. And then rationality reintruded. He could no more make a demand like that than he could muscle past whatever men called that sty their home. He could picture the faces the men would wear, oily, shadowed jaws and hostile, simmering eyes, violence awaiting a single word misplaced. He knew their kind, he'd been raised in this benighted county. Those trailer-park wastrels wouldn't be the first riff raff he'd encountered in his life.

The phone was right there, but to get involved...where might that lead? What explosions of southern indignation might follow? He saw Serendipity so clearly in his mind, such a sweet girl, such a smart girl. She deserved so much more, more than even he could give her let alone those people over there. He snatched the receiver out of its cradle and spun the dial.

They came with sirens from both directions on the highway, sirens at first warbling from far away but one could instinctively tell where they would converge. He listened through his window, he couldn't bear to witness it from his porch, the screams and shouts, the barked orders, the clamor of indignation and reprisal, the sirens shrieking painfully through the air, and the girls...the girls crying as they were taken away.

It was quiet now as autumn came, as the leaves made their gentle, wafting journeys and as the creek flowed again. The place beyond the bushes was as still as a windless day, had been for a while now. It was becoming too cool for afternoons on the porch. Hot coffee had replaced his iced tea, although his newspaper was still the same. Soon he would move inside with the season.

All was quiet, peaceful, and with a sudden, shuddering sob, he wept.

NO PLACE
FOR
THE YOUNG

BUSINESS WAS WAR in the absence of violence.

Grayson Bennet had read that somewhere and it was true. The young man with the sharp chin, pitiless eyes, and hair that flaunted its luster at Grayson and the other old men sitting across the table could as well have been a medieval warrior glaring malevolently over the top of a shield. His was a look that held no mercy, would offer no compromise, and would not relent until the contractual bloodletting was done.

Grayson's partner, Harv Presley, leaned in to whisper in Grayson's ear. "He's a cocky Young Turk, isn't he?"

The lawyers were droning on with their boilerplate nonsense, burning billable hours with applied inefficiency. At least someone would get rich from this disaster. Grayson noticed that the kid, Aiden Cummins, had tuned out the lawyers as well, and was smirking at Grayson the way that same medieval warrior might smirk before plunging a sword into the belly of the enemy king. Grayson covered his mouth to hide his response to Harv, but kept his aged eyes locked on his foe.

"He's a cocky Young Turk with a lot of cash and support. We're going to lose the company. You know that, right?"

"I didn't want to say it."

"Denial won't stop it from happening. The question is, how do we come back at the brat when the dust settles?"

"I don't know. Bed his mom, maybe."

Grayson chuckled, drawing the ire of a gray-suited attorney whom Grayson would never be able to describe once this meeting was over. Law was the field he should have gone into, he thought ruefully, flush with cash, no strain of imagination, and little work beyond perching on a pole and waiting for the next train wreck to occur. "We were never as cocky as that prick," Grayson whispered to Harv.

"Are you kidding? We were worse! Forty years ago we would have run that kid down with our Cadillacs for pulling a stunt like this."

"With our Lincolns, you mean."

"Well, you always were a Ford man."

"Pretty cars back then."

"Yeah, enough room to shake a leg and still cram in a wet bar."

"I miss those days."

"I hear ya, partner."

The meeting concluded with forced smiles and handshakes that hurt. Grayson was rubbing his knuckles as he and Harv walked to the elevator.

"Bastard about broke my hand," Grayson complained.

"Display of dominance," Harv commented.

"And that's what I hate the worst. This wasn't supposed to be zero sum, but that's the way it looks. I guarantee you the board will notice."

"And then the shareholders," Harv added with a pointed look as the elevator door hissed open.

Downstairs in the hotel bar, Grayson sipped a single malt while Harv indulged his fondness for martinis. It was the smaller of the two hotel bars, dark, cramped, and only populated by a few older businessmen in rumpled suits. The bartender was an odd but attractive girl in her twenties, otherwise there wasn't a woman in sight. Both men noticed.

"He's got them all over there," Harv commented dryly. He meant the bigger, brighter bar across the lobby. "Even the more—uhm—*mature* ladies are fawning over the boy. This bar is for the has-beens."

"That's us," Grayson muttered with a rattle of ice. He caught the bartender's eye and nodded for a refill. "I don't know," he went on. "Maybe we should just take the cash and retire."

"That doesn't sound like you," Harv said not quite harshly. "What would you do then? Gardening? Bingo? I'm not ready for that kind of life."

"Yeah, that does sound pretty lame. It might be different if—well, at least you have a wife and a kid."

"Uh, huh, I've got a kid who's forty and still trying to figure out what he wants to do with his life, and a wife who's happiest when I'm not home. No, your judgment was always better than mine. Staying single... you made the right call."

"It seemed like it then, anyway. We were too busy. I don't know how you found the time for a family."

"Such as it is."

Harv drained his martini as the bartender arrived to top off Grayson's glass. "Another for you, too?" she asked Harv, who nodded and slid his glass toward her.

Grayson took a moment to give the bartender a closer look. She seemed familiar for some reason, although she was young enough to have been his granddaughter if he'd gone that route, average height, with bootblack hair in a retro 80s shag, pale complexion, a clever tilt to her lips and a cunning look in her dark eyes. A black leather jacket hung from a hook behind her, and a diamond stud glittered in her right nostril. He was certain that she would have tatts under her white uniform blouse as well—all the kids did these days—and he felt a sudden interest in what they might look like. "What's your name?" he asked her.

She turned that cunning look on him, a look he'd seen more than a few times over the decades. Hairstyles changed, fashions changed, but that look never did. It was a look of shrewdness, of savvy, willing to go a certain distance in order to draw a padded tip, but unwilling to be pushed a step further. It was a look that said this girl could handle herself, especially with balding gray-hairs in dated suits.

"Tangent," she said flatly, as if she had answered that question ten too many times on this day alone.

"C'mon," Grayson grumbled. "What's your real name?"

"Tangent Taylor," she answered this time, adding a deniable hint of sarcasm to her voice.

She spun away then to mix Harv's martini, humming an old tune as she went, a tune that Grayson vaguely recognized but then disregarded when Harv interjected with a laugh, "Strike three, old man."

"Naw, that's not what I was thinking."

"Then you *are* getting too old for this."

"I was just remembering," Grayson said toward the dimly lit bottles behind the bar. "It was exactly like this with us, remember? Just a couple of smart-asses in suits, with a good con and not a dollar between us."

"Yeah," Harv remembered fondly. "You had a way with the bartenders—even the guys. You could *always* talk them out of free drinks. Even now I don't know how you did it."

"Not this girl though," Grayson said in resignation. Tangent was at the mixing station, tapping her foot and singing just loud enough for Grayson to catch a few husky words. *...don't hardly know her...*

"That's only because we're old, we can pay for our own drinks, and she knows it," Harv commented, reclaiming Grayson's full attention.

"Huh." Grayson chuckled. "It really was just like this. No office, no address, no phone—" He glanced sourly at his smart phone lying on the bar, an office on the go that had changed everything. "—so we set up in a hotel, flirted with everybody, made it look like we owned the place."

"Yeah," Harv laughed, caught up in the memory. "You even got that waitress to answer the phone for us. Remember?" He mimed a receiver in his ear. "Bennet-Presley Investments. How may I direct your call?"

Grayson smiled reflectively. "Man, what a bluff that was."

"But it worked."

"Yeah, it did. Do you think that's why we're here? In a hotel, I mean. Do you think Aiden's pulling the same con on us?"

"Hmm...I never thought about it like that." Tangent brought Harv his martini. He thanked her and she left, silently this time.

"We should have thought about it, though. We're supposed to be experienced and wise and—"

"We are, man," Harv cut in, "but damn that kid's good looking. And sharp, too. It's hard to compete with that."

"I was wondering if we could turn it somehow...use it against him, you know?"

"What, his looks?"

"No, his youth."

"Hmm, maybe. It would be easier if we had his hair." Both men laughed.

"It would be easier if we were young again," Grayson muttered morosely.

"Wouldn't it, though? You know, I read something online about that. The Chinese have got some new kind of procedure coming down the pipe. Gene therapy, or something like that."

"It's always the Chinese, isn't it?"

"Seems like it. Man, they were hard to play with."

"I'm just glad we got through that fight with our assets intact."

"It was a close thing for a while there."

"Uh, huh, but we beat 'em. And if we can beat the Chinese then we should damn well be able to beat that prick Aiden."

"A few more of these," Harv held up his martini and grinned, "and we might just figure something out."

The bottom line, Grayson thought, back at his apartment, well after midnight and unable to sleep, was that he had more money than he could ever spend. So why bother with any of this?

His apartment looked down on a frenetic city that never slept, his high castle, held securely in trust until the day he died. He stood at his picture window and watched the city hum and course and flow. There were millions of stories down there, mere traffic patterns in the night and all dreaming of what he had, dreaming well into the gray of their own lives, and none—excepting a rare few—would ever reach his heights. Sometimes it all seemed so futile, such a misdirection of finite energy, but damn if it wasn't galling to lose to the likes of Aiden Cummins!

He caught his reflection in the plate glass, a diaphanous old ghost quavering against the teeming city, and not even fit to haunt it. He never once in his life denied the inevitability of his later, senescent years, he was only taken aback because they'd crept up so incrementally. His hair began to recede in his 30s, while at the same time his belly began to expand. His 40s taught him never to stray far from a restroom, and then in his 50s came the jowly cheeks and flaccid throat, accompanied by odd aches and pains that followed their own inscrutable schedule. The gray first arrived as dignified streaks in the moustache he wore in the 80s, forgotten when he finally shaved that off for good and as his once-bountiful chestnut hair receded farther, only for the gray to reappear in his 50s as a stately dusting at his temples before going on to encompass the entire fringe around his mottled pate.

Not to mention sleeplessness, which was why he was up now, his aggravating and damnably inconvenient farsightedness, the torturous ringing in his ears, and his withering libido, a topic best left unremarked.

His mind was still sharp, though. He sensed no diminution there, only the greater exertion it took to arrive at thoughts that had once come instinctively and at a blink. The hell with the wisdom of elders, he cursed inwardly. Theirs was only a struggle for relevance amid a baggage of memories and in the face of the young, who had the energy to act and to find their own solutions. In truth, although he never denied the ultimate fate he shared with everybody, the reflection he took in now was the hard slap of a reality he simply couldn't believe had actually happened to *him*. Must he surrender to it; must he blithely accept it? Must he surrender to—of all people—*Aiden Cummins*? Was that truly what fate demanded, and could he live with it regardless?

He plodded to his wet bar and poured a gritty measure of single malt. Above the wet bar was his wall screen. He could see his reflection in it, too, a reflection that studied him back as scrupulously as he studied it, an unflattering portrait.

"Penelope, search Chinese gene therapy."

Penelope was his virtual assistant, which he'd renamed from its silly corporate moniker and in honor of a girlfriend he'd had in college, a girlfriend who, in contradiction to Harv's comment at the bar that afternoon, Grayson dearly wished he'd held on to.

The wall screen blinked to life and then scrolled through links, an infinity of them.

"Narrow to aging research."

There were no fewer links, but these were more focused. He stood there, supporting his drinking elbow and reading from link to link. And he was amazed. There was much more activity out there than he ever dreamed, and he berated himself for missing it. A younger man would have caught on early and invested heavily—younger men *had* caught on early and invested heavily—but the entire industry had somehow passed him by. It didn't take him long to glean the crux of it.

"Penelope, what time is it in Shanghai?"

"The current time in Shanghai is 14:53 hours," Penelope answered in her default mezzo-soprano. "Would you like to know the weather?"

"No, that's quite all right." It's afternoon there, he thought. "Penelope, call Zhang Yon."

"Calling Zhang Yon."

Zhang Yon answered after only two rings, a punctiliousness that never failed to startle Grayson. "Grayson, how are you?" the heavily inflected voice asked.

"I'm well, Yon. And you?"

"There is always work to do, and never the hours. But you know this, too."

"Yes, I do," Grayson agreed in commiseration. "So tell me, Yon, am I still persona non grata in Shanghai?"

"You were never persona non grata in China, my old friend, but you did make the authorities—what is the word?—*apprehensive* I believe it is."

"And how are they now?"

"Worried about everything as always, and too busy worrying to worry about you."

"That's good." Grayson's thoughts formed a pensive smile. "So Yon, I want to see if you can set something up for me..."

After more than two years of turmoil flush with profit for the intrepid few (including Grayson), the West had shrugged off the pandemic as if it were nothing more than last year's hurricane. In Shanghai, though, there were still lingering aftereffects. Facemasks were even more profligate than before, now converted into a trendy fashion statement, and there were hand-sanitizing stations every few feet. Otherwise the place was still an anthill, and the air was still foul. Zhang Yon met Grayson at customs and greased him through the bureaucracy. They shook hands warmly.

"Yon, you look...really good."

The two were the same age, but while Grayson looked obese and old, Yon looked wiry and wizened.

"You are looking well also," Yon lied with a grin. The two had met in college and had countless stories between them. The decades hadn't dimmed their bond in the slightest. "And how is Harv?"

"The same as always, busy keeping an eye on things while I'm away."

"That is good." Yon paused in thought; then, "I say again, my friend, that this treatment you seek is still highly experimental."

"I'll take the chance, Yon. I mean...look at me. What have I really got to lose?"

Yon's grin fell. "Your life, my friend."

"I'm not sure I haven't lost that already."

Westerners were always so singularly focused, the source of their strengths but also their weaknesses. Yon shrugged. "As you wish, Grayson, but I will still worry."

"And I appreciate it. So when do we go over there?"

"We go now."

"Good."

The institute was one of those towering glass and chrome edifices that proclaim their presence from far away on clear days. In this yellow smog, though, the building looked more pewter than polished. Yon shuffled Grayson through myriad meetings with lab-coated personnel whose smiles never seemed completely sincere. Grayson had sunk a lot of money into their stock, however, and of that they were well aware. Tens of millions of dollars bought at least the pretense of politeness, and in this case, an off-the-books experimental treatment plan as well. Yon stayed to translate as Grayson disrobed and donned a plain white and uselessly thin medical gown. He was being rushed through, not out of efficiency, he thought, but out of anxiety.

"So you have studied the procedure," Yon translated for the attending, who was so mummied up in PPE that his sing-song voice sounded like an emphatic mumble. "You will enter an induced coma, and will remain in that state for at least one month. Electrodes will prevent atrophy, and will help build the new muscle."

Grayson understood. It was unsettling that he would lay helpless among possibly—if not probably—xenophobic strangers for such a long period, but remaining conscious, he had read, would expose him to excruciating pain for the duration, which would in turn release hormones that would disrupt the lengthening of his telomeres. This was a leap he had to take, not a leap of faith but a leap of rational determination. In other words, he had no choice. He trusted Yon to look after matters, although he relied on more than simply his friend's loyalty. If all went well, Yon would be rewarded with his own turn at the procedure. The opportunity of longevity earned an extra attentiveness that money couldn't buy, although it was money that had made the opportunity possible.

He lay down on a gurney as instructed. The room became a blizzard of activity as IVs were hung and tubes attached. Something cold oozed into his arm, tracing a course to his shoulder and then across his chest. Yon was right there wearing that worried look, and then Grayson closed his eyes and remembered nothing.

His eyes were sticky when he opened them. The room was empty, and the sunlight coming through the windows seemed off, duskier perhaps, as if he had lain for a short nap and had awoken hours later. He scrunched his eyes to focus, was confused by colors too sharp to be anything except imagination. His throat was dry, his spit so syrupy that he couldn't swallow. He felt weak, and yet he was able to sit up without too much effort.

He managed to swing his legs over the side of the bed, went to stand but the tubes in his arms and elsewhere held him back. He shook at the gauze in his head. What was this? Where was he? Too much booze was his first thought, but that always came with a throbbing headache and a sour stomach, and he felt none of that. A red button lay by his side. He pressed it.

In moments, a crowd of doctors swarmed into the room, crowding into the small space and prattling in a language that bore holes into his skull. He waved them back but they pressed in anyway.

"Mr. Bennet," one of them said. "Please to wait first."

Doctors took him firmly by the shoulders and pushed him back into the bed. Someone fiddled with an IV bag, and Grayson drifted off.

When he awoke again he felt much better. His eyes were clear, his mouth was moist, and Zhang Yon was hovering over him with a smile too wide for such a narrow face.

"Grayson, how do you feel?" Yon asked.

Grayson lifted a hand to his forehead and was startled when his fingers raked through bristly hair. "Uh, I feel pretty good, I think."

"Do you know where you are?"

Grayson looked around, squinting at the blazing clarity that met his eyes. "Uh, in a hospital?"

"Yes, very good. And do you know why you are here?"

Grayson had to pause and think, a blank expression as he ran it through his mind. "The procedure," he said slowly; and then with a dawning, "The procedure!"

"Yes. Good. You remember."

Grayson sat up. His medical gown was stained with dried fluids that gave off an unpleasant odor. He flexed his fingers, noticed the brownish hairs between his knuckles, the smooth skin. "Wha—did it work?" he uttered.

"I think you will be very pleased."

Grayson rubbed life into his stubbly face, felt firm cheeks and chin, and skin as elastic as memory. As if not daring to explore further, he returned his hands tentatively to his head, jerked away at the feel of the short, sharp hairs, but then resumed with a widening smile, scratching vigorously.

"For now it is still short," Yon translated for a doctor who wore a disturbingly exaggerated smile, "but your hair will grow back naturally in time."

Grayson's dawning sense of wonder was driven aside by an insistent urgency. "Mirror, man. Mirror!" he all but shouted. This kind of thing happened in movies all the time, but nobody ever thought to have a mirror ready?

Yon translated the command to the doctors, who had their faces un-covered and were standing in a tight line as if up for review. Their broad smiles wilted until a mirror was procured, and then their smiles broad-ened once more as they waited with abated breath for the verdict from their patient. "Here you are, my friend," Yon said. "I am very jealous of you now."

Grayson snatched the mirror impatiently, but then hesitated. With a swallow, and an Adam's apple that hadn't bobbed so prominently in decades, he looked into the glass. "My God—"

"You have been under for seven weeks," Yon continued to translate.

"Longer than expected, but your prognosis is good."

Grayson touched his jaw with disbelieving fingers.

"You could use a shave, my friend," Yon said with a touch of mirth.

Grayson lowered the mirror to his lap and looked up with a strained expression on his newly-handsome face, and then his eyes filled and he bent over, sobbing.

"What is it, Grayson? What is the matter?" Yon had an arm around Grayson's shuddering shoulders as the doctors moved in, their smiles wiped away in an instant. Grayson held up a hand to ward them off.

"It's nothing," he sniffed. He knuckled his eyes and patted Yon's hand. "It's...it's..." The tears returned. "I forgot how beautiful it was," he sobbed out. "I didn't even know it was gone, but now...now I can see that it was. I can *feel* that it was." He never appreciated how well and vigorous he felt when he was young, so long ago that age had overwritten those memories with the practical imperatives of the moment. It was almost tragically sad to be able to compare the two now. He shook his head in grief. "So many years..."

"It is all well now, my friend," Yon consoled him, patting Grayson's back as if Grayson were a child, and wondering if he himself would experience this shock when it was his turn.

Grayson's discharge from the institute was almost comically anticlimactic, no protocols to adhere to, no regimen to follow, no drugs to take. The doctors waved and bowed in obsequious success, their smiles no less insincere. The only perplexing issue was the way his clothes now hung on him like beggars' rags, an issue quickly resolved when Yon sprinted off to pick up some more appropriate items.

Grayson said goodbye to his dear friend at the airport. Yon winced as they shook hands, and Grayson winced with guilt.

"Will you go through with it right away?" Grayson asked then. "Or will you wait?" He owed Yon everything, but he couldn't help but draw away slightly from an old man who seemed like little more than a dreary, desiccated husk.

"Soon, I should think," Yon answered tiredly.

"Good." Grayson patted Yon gently on the shoulder. "I'll be back to help you. Just call."

Grayson's flight in First Class offered every amenity: single malt from an actual bottle and in an actual glass, broadband, and a perky stewardess with a mischievous mouth. He smiled lasciviously and set that aside for later. They would be hours in the air yet. He booted up his laptop instead and got in touch with Harv.

"So let's see you," Harv said in a voice more breathy than Grayson remembered.

"Can't, pal. There's something wrong with my computer. I don't know what." In truth, Grayson had closed his camera window on purpose, and he wasn't sure why. He could see Harv, though, a dowdy old man who triggered a repellent pang somewhere in the pit of Grayson's stomach.

"Well, you'll be here soon enough. So here's the deal: Aiden got control of the board while you were under, just like we thought he would. He's selling off assets like crazy and paying them out as dividends. There won't be much left if we don't move fast."

"Do you have any ideas about that?"

"Nothing firm enough to mention. I've been waiting on you."

And that was the problem with old people, Grayson thought dimly, their proclivity to procrastinate when time demanded action.

"Okay, I'll go over the material you sent. I've still got what, fourteen hours in the air? We'll put something together."

"Good. In the meantime, we're bringing you in as Cliff Bennet, your grandnephew."

"I don't have a grandnephew named Cliff."

"You do now. We've done all the paperwork and background. You have officially retired and turned control of your shares over to him. I can't wait to see what happens when you walk into that boardroom."

"It should certainly be interesting."

"Maybe you can just challenge Aiden to a fistfight and settle it that way."

Grayson chuckled even though he didn't think it was that funny. "We'll see. Gotta go, Harv. See you soon."

Grayson signed off before Harv could reply, snapped his laptop closed and then turned his attention toward his perky stewardess.

Grayson rebooked the final leg of his flight online once he'd finished with the stewardess, whose name was...well, it didn't matter. He'd rebooked to avoid the gawping, gawking reception he would have received from Harv. He would have to find a way to ease into that reunion.

The city was dark when his plane landed, and damp. The runway was slick, the lights mere orbs of gauze. Fog was billowing over the waterfront, probing the canyoned streets from block to city block, joining and oozing onward, like a biblical breath. Grayson hunched his shoulders into it, hailed a taxi and had it take him home.

The doorman was wary, but also wise enough not to confront a suit that well-tailored and a Rolex that prominent. Grayson signed *Cliff Bennet* into the register, and then went on up.

His apartment was quiet and smelled odd. He grimaced at the dated furnishings, at all the shellacked wood and oriental lighting and plush carpet. He made a mental note to redecorate as soon as possible.

"Penelope," he said, "install new user."

"User name?"

"Cliff Bennet."

"Access level?"

"Administrative."

"Verify code."

Grayson gave Penelope the code as he went to pour himself a drink. At least the single malt still hit the spot, he thought in relief. He also gave a thought to changing Penelope's name, but nixed that when the memory of his lost love appeared as if she were with him in the here and now. He swore he could feel her warmth, taste her lips. No, he would let Penelope be.

He took his drink to the picture window, looked down on the shrouded city and pondered his next move, which wasn't apparent but it would come, of that he was certain, as certain as he was that he would take Aiden out, and that he would do it as brutally as possible.

He caught his reflection in the glass, and this time studied it with wry appreciation. No ghost haunted this image. His face was angular and firm, his apparent age about twenty-five or so. He'd intended to shave off the stubble as soon as he got home, but now he saw in it an appealing, rakish quality. Combined with his military-style short hair, his was a look of confidence, of strength and masculinity that fit in with current trends perfectly, a look he decided to keep for a while, a new persona for a new life filled with all the experience but none of the baggage of the previous.

He paused those thoughts, suddenly distracted by the silence in his apartment, an all-encompassing stillness that was disturbing in its depth. He tilted his ears first this way and then that trying to puzzle it out. He lived too high above the streets for any of that noise to make it this far, so that wasn't what was missing. He focused harder and detected a subtle thrum in one wall, a sound he'd never noticed before, and then it came to him and he inhaled sharply in recognition. The ringing in his ears, the shrill static he'd endured for years, was gone. Of course!

He was awed anew by the marvelous, manifold changes in his perception, but the overpowering silence also revealed a hollowness that cried out to be filled.

"Penelope, play some background sounds."

"This is a request not in memory. Please specify a preference."

"Uh, ocean sounds. Soft."

"Playing *Gentle Waves*."

The sound of a languid summer sea dabbled ever so lightly in his ears, washing into the far corners of the apartment with calm and serenity but bringing him little comfort. It was more than an absence of sound, the hollowness. He needed something to touch as well. Or someone. This was a need that crowded business concerns from the forefront of his mind, and then an old tune found its way into his thoughts and he knew what he was going to do.

"Penelope, play music."

"Specify genre and period."

He smiled, slyly, the way he always smiled when a plan came together.

"Send an email to Harv first: 'Something's come up. I'll be delayed a few days. Be in touch soon.'"

"Email sent."

"Good. Now Penelope, play songs by Joan Jett..."

A lubricated phone call to a corporate lackey confirmed her schedule, so he knew exactly when to arrive. For clothing, he'd had Penelope search through the current styles of comfortable, informal, but not slovenly dress, and had arrived at expensive jeans and a long-sleeved cream waffle shirt under a collared, dark purple outer shirt left unbuttoned. He wore no watch, and kept his phone in a back pocket.

The bar was as dark as before. The few loitering businessmen looked the same, albeit these many weeks older. Grayson took a seat at the bar and noted the black leather jacket hanging on its hook. Tangent approached him skeptically.

"You lost?" she asked.

"No, just looking for someplace quiet."

"Well, you found it. What'll you have?"

Grayson smiled sheepishly, stood and pulled out his empty pockets. "I'm not sure."

"I am," Tangent said in disgust, and she turned away.

"Wait," Grayson said hastily. "Certainly we can work something out."

Tangent turned back on him with a venomous expression. "You can haul your ass downtown for that kind of sh—"

"No, I'm terribly sorry. That's not what I meant."

She now wore the dubious look of impatience edging toward the end of a long shift. "Then what *did* you mean? And you talk funny, by the way."

"I'm not from around here."

"No kiddin'."

"No kidding," he smiled.

Tangent ran her tongue into a cheek and took a step toward him. "Okay, I'm curious," she said, "so go ahead and tell me your story."

"There's not much to tell. I sure could use a drink, though."

"Not with empty pockets you don't."

"What if...hmm."

She took a step closer. "What if what?"

"Uhm, what if I could guess your favorite song? Would you trade me a drink for that?"

She laughed. "Man, you are really full of it. That's not even a long-shot, that's just stupid."

"But what if I could do it?"

She rolled her eyes. "And what do I get when you're wrong."

"I'll leave."

"That's something I can look forward to, then."

"So what about it?"

"Okay," she sighed. "Tell you what: you guess my favorite song and I'll give you *two* free drinks, but when you're wrong you get out like right now, got it?"

"Got it."

"Well?"

"Hmm," he rubbed his chin, still enjoying the novelty of his nascent beard, "let me see." He looked her up and down as if gleaning clues. "It would have to be something slow and fast at the same time, am I right?"

"What? You think I'm going to tell you?"

"And guitars. Good guitar work." His brows lifted while hers dropped.

"Go on."

"Hmm." He gave her a last look-over, and then grinned with his rejuvenated teeth. "I think it would have to be *Crimson and Clover*, the Joan Jett & the Blackhearts version?"

Tangent's face fell in disbelief. "No effin way!"

"So I'm right then?"

"You can't know that. What's the scam?"

"No scam, but a single malt over ice would be nice."

"I don't believe this."

"Believe your ears."

"Okay, dammit," she stamped in disgust. "I got Glenlivet and Glenfiddich."

"Glenlivet will do."

Grayson had forgotten how fun it could be to banter with a stranger this way, whether or not it led to anything more. Sex was a point but not always the point, just the interaction, the test of wills was enough. But this girl Tangent—she had something. She brought him his Glenlivet over ice and lingered, as he knew she would. Curiosity and intrigue were traits too many people did not possess. If she had walked away, he would have walked away as well.

"So what's your name?" he asked her.

"Tangent Taylor," she answered tightly but ungrudgingly.

"Cool name."

"I like it. So what's yours?"

"Gra—Cliff Bennet."

"Weird name, Graycliff. So what do you do?"

"I make money."

She held him with a dubious look. "Empty pockets and all?"

"My pockets are empty, but I didn't say my bank account was."

She eyed him with the reevaluating look he also expected, the one in which she admitted to herself that she might have read this wrong from the start. "Bank account, huh?"

"That's right," he said. "And you..." he looked around. "This doesn't seem like the kind of place for a Joan Jett aficionado."

"It's the best kind of place," she said sharply. "I make a ton of tips off these guys. Dive bars are full of poor people. This is where the money is, am I right?"

"It's where I am."

She came in close and leaned on an elbow. "So let's talk about that."

During his younger, rollicking decades, Grayson had acquainted himself intimately with not too few fashionable socialites and no less few Hollywood celebrities, but none of them could compare to a night with Tangent.

She was still groggy with sleep, while he was wide-awake and ready to resume. She wriggled at his ticklish touch as he traced the tatt on her pale belly, rolling over on her side and now he could trace the tatt in the small of her back. She also had a tatt on the inside of her creamy thigh, an orchid, as well as a circle of runic symbols around her right bicep. Grayson had never been inked, but was rethinking that now.

He got up and padded to her bathroom, where he let vent in a fount more deeply satisfying than any he had experienced in four decades, and again he felt the melancholy and injustice of the aging process. When the procedure was refined and released into the mainstream, the profits were going to be enormous. He was well positioned for that eventuality. In the meantime, finding a partner whose mind could keep up was going to be the challenge, a challenge he was fairly sure he'd already overcome.

Tangent came up behind him trailing a sheet wrapped around her hips. She was bare from the navel up, and damn if that wasn't sexy as hell. He felt the stir, and a fullness that hadn't shown itself since the last time he was twenty-five. Tangent reached around and embraced him, fingers questing.

"Well, you're ready," she said, breathing onto his shoulder.

"And you're beautiful."

She nipped his skin with sharp teeth. "And you're insatiable and I'm really sore."

"Sorry about that."

She grinned against his skin. "Have you been stranded on an island or something?"

"No, just too busy with business...which I'm going to have to get back to pretty soon."

She exhaled. "Right."

"No," quickly, "that's not what I meant. I could use your help."

She was rubbing her cheek between his shoulder blades now. "What do I have to do?"

"Help me take a guy down."

She pushed him away. "Something illegal?"

"No, not in the least, but something with a good pay-out if it works."

That got her attention. She drew him back to the bed, rolled over on top and pressed his shoulders into the pillow. "So tell me about it then."

"Let me gather my thoughts," he grinned, and she grinned in return.

Harv wasn't happy. They were in Grayson's apartment, it was late afternoon, and the sun was just beginning to shed soft light. Harv wanted to extoll, be amazed and slap his friend on the back, but the presence of the sultry, leather-jacketed girl in the corner chair forced him to hold his tongue. She seemed familiar but he couldn't place her.

"So, uh, Cliff," he said uncertainly.

"This is Tangent, by the way," Grayson diverted. He wrinkled his nose. Harv smelled gassy, something Grayson never noticed before.

"She's going to help us with our, uh, business problem."

Harv's brows arched in vague recognition, but then fell into a perplexed frown. "Help us?"

Grayson gestured Harv over to the wet bar. "Penelope, play songs by Joan Jett & the Blackhearts."

"Playing Joan Jett & the Blackhearts."

Tangent jumped up with a grin and danced in place, while Grayson mixed a martini for his friend. The music beat painfully at Harv's ears, but Grayson seemed unperturbed.

"The plan," Grayson said in a low voice, forcing Harv to lean in to hear, "is for Tangent to get in close to Aiden, and she can do it, believe me."

Harv found himself shouting even though Grayson could have heard him fine anyway. "And do what?" he asked.

"Nothing except distract him at the right time."

"Does she—uh—does she know about you?" Harv was simply startled beyond belief by his friend's physical condition, a condition he remembered so well but from so long ago. He felt a pang of jealousy, then worse, a pang of irrelevance.

"Only that I'm Cliff Bennet. That's enough for now."

"So how are we going to take him down?"

"I'm still working on that."

"Grayson, I..." There was a wounded look in Harv's tired eyes. "I thought it would be just me and you, you know? Together like before. I don't even know this girl."

"She's good, old man" Grayson reassured him, "and we need the help. Just sit tight until it's time. You'll be there, I promise."

"If you say so, but it still doesn't feel right."

Grayson poured himself a single malt and then moved away from Harv's smell. "That'll do it for now," he said loud enough for Tangent to hear. "Drink up, Harv, and we'll get together again soon."

Harv knew he was being dismissed, and the hurt showed. He downed his martini in a single gulp and then ushered himself to the door.

After Harv left, Tangent took Grayson's hand and pulled him to the center of the floor. *Crimson and Clover* had just come on. "Let's dance," she said breathlessly.

"I'm not very good at it," Grayson warned her. His dancing prowess leant itself to more sedate music.

"Who cares?"

So they danced, slowly at first and with arms around each other, but then leaping into a frenetic tempo as the guitars came in. Soon they were only jumping in place, and Grayson was having the time of his life.

Tangent was curious about Harv. "So who is he, a friend of your Dad's or something?"

"An old friend, yes."

"And he works for you?"

"No, we're partners."

"He's your *partner*?"

"Yeah, a good numbers man."

"He smells."

"He can't help it."

"I had a grandfather once. Reminds me of him."

"Did you like your grandfather?"

"He was okay, just stuck in the past, you know? Kinda like your apartment. I mean, your place is really dope, but it's got this *Mad Men* thing goin' on. Know what I mean?"

"Yeah," Grayson laughed. That was the perfect description of him and Harv, mad men, but Grayson didn't intend to live that way a second time. "I know what you mean. I really need to redecorate."

"Ya think?"

It was easy to lose the days with Tangent, days he marked no more than he marked the beating of his heart. She was a boundless store of ideas and desires, all rooted in the reality of a congested world displaced by degrees from the effete world he and his kind had manufactured in order to keep themselves wealthy. Crossings between the two worlds were common enough in literature and film, and in life as well. Dalliances occurred daily, now, before, and probably forever, but Grayson wondered if Tangent might be more than that.

Her long shifts at the bar were excruciating for him. He would stop in to see her, to revel in her authenticity. Tangent might be footloose and living in the moment, but she wasn't flippant or frivolous, nor was she idling her time away.

"The pandemic messed up my plans," she told him one afternoon. The bar was seldom busy, so their conversations often had the time to range widely. "But I'm back on track now."

"How so?"

"I've always wanted to travel, to see the world, you know? I have friends who did it. They got enough money together somehow, and they flew to Spain. They didn't plan anything, they just took off. They crashed at hostels and squatted in empty flats, and when they needed money they stomped grapes and picked artichokes, and after a while they moved on somewhere else. They sent me postcards and selfies. I envied them, man, they were so effin free—until they ran out of money and got stuck in Bangkok. They had to do some nasty things to get out of there. I sure didn't envy them then."

Grayson had already seen the world, of course, from 40,000 feet and from penthouse views, from the finest restaurants with the finest porcelain and with people tripping over themselves to show him a good time. He knew the world, but he did not know the world Tangent was describing.

He was sitting at the end of the bar, his chin resting in his palm, listening to Tangent talk while she dried glasses with a dishtowel. She continued:

"So I still want to see the world, but not just the ugly part of it like they did. You know what I mean?" Grayson nodded. "And that takes money. I finally saved enough to open a brokerage account online. I invested some in index funds and the rest in pharma and green energy."

"Where'd you learn to do that?" Grayson asked, plainly astonished.

"YouTube," she said as if it were self-evident. "Where'd you learn?"

Grayson snorted. "Princeton."

"Figures. I think I got the better deal."

Grayson noted the competition in her words, and responded as he would with anybody who threw down a gauntlet like that. "I don't know, I think I've done pretty well. I've gotten you to give me free drinks, after all."

She gave him her sly smile. "Yeah, and I've gotten you to give me big tips."

Grayson opened his mouth for a wry rebuttal, but there wasn't one. "Good point," he said instead, and they both laughed. "So what happened with the pandemic?" he asked. "I mean, the market boomed right through that, especially pharma if you stayed away from those oxy morons. You should have made it out in great shape."

"No work," she said. "All the bars were locked down—and it takes a while to build up enough capital to compound it in the market. C'mon, you know that."

In truth, he did, but he had become so inured in success for so long that it had come to seem preordained, as if his and Harv's struggles decades back had been an obvious and guaranteed thing.

"Yes, of course I do," he said after he'd mulled those thoughts.

Tangent gave him a skeptical eye. "I'm not so sure about that."

"What? Are you jealous or something?"

"Why should I be? I've got my own gig, man, and I'll get where I wanna be with or without you."

This came heated, and shaped into a slap that stung, a slap that reminded Grayson that Tangent was not a waif needing rescue, but a tough gal who could slug above her weight. And damn he could love her for that. "I'm sorry," he said. "I can see what you're accomplishing for yourself. I'm just thinking maybe I can help you get there faster."

"And I'll take the ride," she came back, still with an edge in her voice, "but I'm not hangin' on anybody's arm."

What had started so casually had escalated into a test he hadn't anticipated. She was that rare, and he would not risk losing her. "I'm not looking for an ornament," he said with just enough bite to let her know he was serious. "I'm looking for a partner who can make things happen."

She allowed a smile, whether devious or delighted he couldn't tell. "Then I'm your girl," she said.

Harv was even less happy now. He had been forced to sit and twiddle his thumbs while Aiden was stoking a fire sale and while Grayson, Harv's best friend, was cavorting like a horny teenager with some trim he'd picked up in a bar. Harv didn't want to sound desperate, he wanted to sound mad. In truth he was both. He called Grayson when these thoughts finally reached a head.

"Dammit, man, why are you wasting time?" Harv barked into the phone.

"Settle down, Harv," Grayson barked in return. It was getting harder and harder for him to remember how close the two had once been. "I'm not wasting time, we're just not there yet."

"That's bull, Grayson, and you know it. We sent you over there so you could come back and get this guy." *We*, Grayson thought acidly. "And so far nobody's even heard of Cliff Bennet. They all think Grayson's hiding out and licking his wounds, and they're turning on us, man. They're turning on us."

"And what do you think?" Grayson asked with forced calm.

"Speak up, man. I can't hear you."

"Then hold your damn ear closer to the phone. I asked what *you* thought."

That was yet another rebuke that went deep. "What I think," Harv spat through gritted teeth, "is that you're infatuated with this...this *girl*, and that you're letting everything else go."

"Harv," Grayson said, barely contained, "that *girl* is my friend."

"I thought I was your friend."

"I wonder about that sometimes."

Harv was so shocked he couldn't speak, he couldn't respond, he couldn't form a thought. He thumbed their connection off and fell back in his chair as if a knife had been driven through his heart.

Harv met with Aiden the next day. There was only one company left that Aiden hadn't touched, and Harv held enough shares to tip the balance Aiden's way.

"I don't need your shares," Aiden said smugly, although in truth this was the break he'd been hoping for. Grayson was a loser, so was Harv, but at least Harv had the sense to take the cash and run. The question was how to drive the price down. "I'll get them cheap enough, soon enough."

"You won't get a better deal unless you work with me directly."

"We'll see about that."

And again Harv was dismissed by a young prick, and that caught in his craw but he had to play his part regardless.

"Your job," Grayson told Tangent that same day, "is to take a job at the main bar."

"What? Aw, man, that place sucks. There are, like, six bartenders over there all trying to be top dog. And they make you divide your tips, man. I make better money here. And besides, they wouldn't even hire me over there if I looked like Ariana Grande."

"They *will* hire you, and you'll be getting the call sometime today."

Tangent bristled. "So you're telling me where I have to work now?"

Grayson smiled patiently, a fatherly aspect he managed to project, and one she found both perturbing and disturbing. He waved for calm as she huffed with her arms tightly crossed. "I have some ideas we should talk about," he said.

Aiden lived in the hotel's penthouse, and kept a coterie of sycophants who ensured his prominence wherever he went. Sometimes, though, they could be so suffocating and droll that he couldn't bear them another instant. At those times he would slip down to the bar by himself to get away, an escape that was more regular than he realized and which had not gone unnoticed. His drink was a vodka tonic. Scotch and martinis were for the gray-hairs.

"Vodka tonic, Mr. Cummins?" Tangent fawned as if he were the center of her world.

"You got it," he said.

He followed her with his eyes as she went to the mixing station. She was a good-looking girl, he thought, with an exotic quality that intrigued him, and a body to match. Her uniform wasn't flattering, but her tight black pants revealed everything he needed to know. She brought him his drink, and he appraised her and made sure she noticed.

"How long you been working here?" he asked.

"Not long."

"You get good tips?"

"Sometimes."

He gave her his chiseled grin and slid a hundred-dollar bill across the bar. "Keep it," he said, "and keep 'em coming."

She arched a brow at such undisguised arrogance, but then hid the hundred in the waist of her pants, first looking furtively to the left and right. Most of the patrons put the tab on their rooms, where their tips were documented and divided later. Cash was a rare, concealable windfall.

"Thanks," she said.

"So what's your name?" he asked.

"Tangent."

"That's a weird name."

She exhaled at the tedium of that remark, but hid it with a professional smile. "It's the one they gave me."

He took a sip and swished it around his gums as if it were fine wine. "Good job." He toasted her with his glass. "You've got skills."

"Thanks." This guy was as smarmy as they came. No wonder Cliff despised the guy. She kept those thoughts hidden as well. "So what do you do?" she asked.

"I make money."

"We all make money."

"But some of us make more of it than others." He was leering over his drink, and it was all she could do not to slap that leer off his face.

"And some people just say that to impress others."

"And some people really mean it."

"Good for you." Another patron was signaling now. "I gotta go."

"Wait." He drained his drink. "I'm ready for another."

She sighed and took his glass. "I'll be right back."

"Of course you will," he said to her back.

Vodka was fun to work with. Flavorless, it could be doubled up in the lemon and tonic and none would be the wiser. After a couple of these, Aiden was slurring and Tangent was leaning close on her elbows as if every word he said had a place in stone. The other bartenders were eyeing her grudgingly, but all of them knew who Aiden was, and that there was a line they dare not cross if he'd taken an interest in the new girl.

"It's funny you mention that," she said after one of his long-winded and rambling expositions. "There was a guy in here the other day, an old guy looking for a buyer. He said he wanted to dump some stock."

That sobered Aiden a measure. "What kind of stock?"

"Hmm, pharma, I think he said. Something about the corona vaccines, a new broad-spectrum single-dose one they can make in bulk."

Aiden straightened up further. "Did you get his name?"

Tangent shook her head in thought. "No, but I saw him come off the elevator. He'd been up top, I think. Maybe he lives up there."

That sent Aiden to his feet. He slid another hundred across the bar. "Thanks," he said. "Later."

"So how'd it go?" Grayson asked her when she got home that evening. They were at her place, which felt like a comfortable old coat to Grayson. He liked her apartment, small and cluttered though it was, and despite the seismic bumps that sometimes sounded from the floor above.

"I think we got his attention."

"Good. Now if he just does what I think he'll do."

"About that—" Grayson was sitting in her worn comfy chair. She sidled over casually and leaned a hip against his shoulder. "—I could make a side bet in this, couldn't I?"

Grayson tensed a little. "What do you mean?"

"I mean—" She was running a coy finger around his ear now. He knew what she was up to, but just the same he didn't want her to stop. "—that stock's gonna take off like crazy. I could make a buy right now." She nodded toward her laptop.

"Yes you could," he said with a sigh, "but that would be insider trading. As a small operator you might get away with it, but in the dust-up that might be coming, I wouldn't take the chance."

"So that's it then?" she asked, deflating at the obvious truth of what he'd said. "We have to sit here and do nothing?"

"We're just along for the ride at this point." He gave her a look that made her heart pick up a beat. "But we don't have to do nothing."

She returned his look just as intently, and his heart sped up a beat as well. She straddled his lap and gave him an inscrutable smile. He was wrong about the ride. They still had the wheel for a little while, but he was right about not having to do nothing, for tonight at least.

Aiden was as equally adept at the lubricated phone call as Cliff was.

Now when he came down he had one end of the long oval bar reserved for himself, and one bartender to serve him. Tangent would have rolled her eyes at the effrontery if a dozen other eyes weren't jealously watching her all the time.

He came out of the elevator immaculately dressed and with an abundance of high-class bling, an extravagant exhibition of excess. Tangent started mixing his drink, and had it ready when he smugly took his seat at the bar.

"Here you go," she said.

He gave her a smile he thought of as irresistible, while she remarked inwardly that he used way too much gel in his hair. He savored a sip, then set his glass down and crossed his arms, fixing her with a gaze that was intent and expectant. She would have felt antsy if she hadn't seen that look countless times on countless faces. Instead she was bored and struggling not to show it.

"So," she said, hoping to snap him back to reality, "did you find that old guy who was selling?"

"Yeah, we worked a deal." His thin lips curled into a smirk that begged to be punched. "You should let me take you out and buy you a drink to celebrate."

"It's your celebration, not mine. And I've got all the drinks I need."

"C'mon," he reached for her possessively.

"Hey!" she jerked away.

"Whoa there, I didn't mean anything." He picked up his drink and went all suave. "Really, though—what'll it take to see you after you get off work?"

"More than you'd be willing to do."

He eased into that opening. "Let me decide that."

She paced as if in indecision; finally, "Then help me get a piece of this pharma deal."

"I could and I would, but that's not where you want to go."

"Why not?"

"Because that stock's gonna tank."

"How do you know that?"

"Because it's what I do."

"That doesn't make sense. If the stock's gonna tank, why do you want it?"

"That would go over your head." He finished his drink and pushed the glass toward her.

"Another?"

"Sure."

She turned their conversation to banal topics, peppered with enough innuendo to keep him interested. After his third drink he was finally dizzy enough for her to venture redirecting him to the point in question.

"So let me see if I've got this right," she said. "You buy short, and when the stock tanks you snap it all up and then repay your creditors with shares? Is that the way it works?"

His brows fluttered and he looked up at her drowsily. "Did I tell you that?"

"Sure you did," she lied. "Why else would we be talking about it?"

"Oh." He circled a finger in a wet ring on the bar. "Yeah—okay—uh, yeah, that's right."

"So when's this going to happen?"

"Tomorrow morning."

"How can you know that?"

"Shh," he held a woozy finger to his lips. "Trade secret."

She wanted to laugh in his face, but instead she signaled at one of his guys, who was sitting bored in a padded chair near the elevator.

"I think he needs to go lay down for a while," she told the guy, and then she snatched off her apron, walked around the bar and told the manager that she quit.

Grayson worried that he might be recognized. There were other old-timers on the board besides Harv, people who would remember the old days. Grayson's thickening beard should hide that, he hoped, as well as his short hair. It was a chance he had to take.

The opening bell that morning had shown once again that greed more often got in the way of good sense. He had called the emergency board meeting, and now he strode into a room of confused and confounded looks, except for Harv, who kept his eyes on his hands.

"Who are you?" Aiden asked from his chair at the head of the table.

Grayson smiled wolfishly. "I'm Cliff Bennet, Grayson Bennet's grandnephew. I have his proxy. Here's the documentation."

He let the paper drift onto the table in front of the secretary, then took a seat and leaned back insouciantly. Aiden had his mouth open to object, but closed it when the secretary nodded after examining the document. "We have a quorum," the secretary said.

"Okay, then," Aiden flicked an impatient glance at his watch, "we have a quorum. So why are we here?"

"One of the board members called an emergency session," the secretary informed him.

"So what's the emergency?"

"The emergency," Grayson spoke up, gazing at his fingernails and seeming more interested in them than in Aiden, "is that the last solid company in our portfolio has devalued sixty percent since the opening bell."

"And why is that an emergency?" Aiden asked flippantly, sensing the subtle challenge from this new guy and needing to brush it off right away.

"It's an emergency," Grayson answered, still more interested in his fingernails, "because that company is our cash cow. You all know this." Some of the board members were eyeing him with phantom recollection, as if he were someone who had leapt out of their past but they couldn't quite place him. "And a company that was on the verge of releasing a profitable new vaccine before—and this was unfortunate—the FDA delayed their approval."

"So what?" Aiden threw up his hands and laughed off the problem. "Stocks go up and down, and the FDA couldn't find the pointed end of a syringe if you showed them. This will blow over like it always does."

"Except that this time—" Grayson now met the eyes of each board member in turn, ending with Aiden, whom he dismissed as if the man were an amateur, "—we have lost our controlling shares, which means that our shareholders are going to be out for blood and that we can't afford this idiot's hobbies anymore."

There were gasps all around. Aiden jumped up and slapped the table. "Who the hell do you think you are?" he growled.

"Just a concerned shareholder," Grayson answered as if Aiden were a petulant child. He turned his attention to the board members, including Harv, who was now looking at him with gray eyes. "It seems that our controlling shares were used in a short-sell, and are being snapped up right now by a holding company that, well," he turned to Aiden, "you know who owns that company, don't you, Aiden?"

"That's bull—"

"Language, Aiden," Grayson chided him. "There are grownups in the room." He turned his focus back on the board members and went on gloomily. "By the end of the day, that holding company will own a majority of the shares, and we won't have enough left between us to make coffee."

Aiden glowered at Grayson, then straightened himself and addressed the board. "You've seen shareholder value increase well beyond market expectations since I took over, and the dividends have been generous, so trust what you know and not some new guy that none of us has even met before."

A few of the board members were nodding, as to be expected. "Let me remind you," Grayson said, standing now, "of the company Harv Presley and my uncle built, based on solid management and solid long-term returns. Stability, people, is what Bennet-Presley Investments is about, not chaos and short-term gains. Without stability we don't have a company, we have a card game."

Aiden clapped derisively. "Good speech, but it's not your uncle's company anymore, or Harv's either. Not now." Harv looked away guiltily. "There's money to be made by those of us who are willing to be aggressive and take chances. The old guard had their day, and those days are over."

"No, I don't think so, Aiden," Grayson said, and then the doors burst open to a flood of FBI agents.

"Aiden Cummins, you're under arrest for insider trading," one of them announced. They read him his rights as they bent him over the table and cuffed him. The board members were frozen in their seats, their jaws in their laps. Grayson stood back with his arms crossed, watching it all play out. Tangent came into the room, dressed elegantly in black, an unaccustomed fashion for her but she was beginning to like it.

"You!" Aiden spat. "You did this!" She gave him her most cunning smile, then smirked and waved as he was led out of the room.

The aftershock was still on their faces when Grayson walked up to the head of the table.

"It's time we get back to what we do best," he said to them. "This company needs solid, experienced leadership. Grayson Bennet has retired, as you know, but we still have Harv Presley. I move that we immediately appoint Harv Presley as interim chairman of the board, to be confirmed at the next shareholder meeting. Any objections?"

"Second," a hand went up.

"Then let's make it unanimous, people, and let's get back to work making money."

Harv came up to Grayson after the meeting had adjourned. Tangent had drifted off, sensing they needed privacy.

"It really hurt for a while there, Grayson."

"I know. It hurt me, too."

"Why couldn't you just tell me from the beginning?"

"Because I wasn't sure it could work, Harv, and if not for Tangent and her recorder, it wouldn't have."

"I was wrong about her. She's a smart girl."

"As smart as they come."

"Have you told her?"

"No."

"Why not?"

"Because I want us to be equals. If she knew, that would always be out there, not obvious maybe, but I would always be the older man with the young girl on his arm. That's the way she would see it, and she wouldn't be wrong."

"You're right," Harv said thoughtfully. "I can see that. And I appreciate what you've done, but I wish you'd stay. I'm not sure I can do it alone."

"Of course you can, Harv. You always could, I was just in your way." Harv shrugged at that, and then the two embraced, with lingering pats on the back and a lifetime of memories passing between them. "Take care of yourself, old man."

"I wish I could say the same."

"Just get the company back on its feet then go see Yon. You've still got plenty of time."

"I'll do that," Harv smiled, then he went off to corral his loyal board members and start setting things right.

Tangent toed her way back to him, her hands clasped in the small of her back and a devious look on her face. "So where do you want to go first?" she asked.

"Are you paying?" he asked, no idea what his liquidity looked like at the moment. "Because I might be broke for a little while."

"Yeah," she laughed, "I can pay. I did pretty well in the market today."

"Uh, hmm, about that—"

"About nothing. Don't worry, I did my buy through a third party so I'm covered. Other than that, my business is my business."

"Point taken. Then in that case, I think I'd like to try stomping some grapes."

She smiled cheerily at that and took his arm. "Then let's go."

Grayson took a parting look around the place he and Harv built, a relic of a former life. It would be decades or even never before more than a privileged few could afford the procedure, and most of those would fall back into the patterns of their former lives, the single-minded drive to acquire more than they would ever need.

But not him. The procedure couldn't be repeated indefinitely because of introduced and unpredictable mutations. For all he knew, this was his one and only second chance at youth. And youth was a gift, not an obligation. Structure, conformity, regimentation—all the vises clamped on people to keep them moving in a certain direction were practical enough when a life was half used up, but that was no place for the young.

MEMORIAM

I HAVE NEVER experienced nostalgia. I have no concept of it. This is not to say that I don't entertain a fond memory from time to time, only that I don't have to plumb deeply to find it. My memories remain in the forefront of my mind, always, like loops of film scrolling endlessly. My fonder memories are right there, whether they be recent or far in the past. My darker memories reside with them side-by-side, inseparable.

In a blink I am three, twenty-three, forty-three, sixty-three.

At three I was alone but not lonely. I reveled in the sun, my world was boundless, and I explored it with a naive innocence propelled by conscious determination. Barely more than a toddler, I would look well up our sunny southwestern street and see something that intrigued me, perhaps a particular palm tree that stood out from the rest or a glint of sun off a discarded toy—it could be anything. And so I would set out to bring it closer, the asphalt hot and sticky on my bare feet, distance only a measure of commitment. I wandered into unlikely places, setting the adults a-panic, but I was never lost. I knew exactly where I was going.

This behavior vexed my mother, who went to ever-more elaborate lengths to keep me corralled at home. Soon came chain-link fences and gates, easily overcome, and eventually a dog that would bark if I ventured beyond a certain point. That dog was a Doberman named Dancer. I remember him as clearly as anything I did yesterday. I remember the suspicious look in his eye as I neared the fence, the toothy bark that would follow, and the powerful solidness of his head when he would nuzzle me away from my goal. I remember his remorseful whine when I learned to leap over him and onto the fence, well above his reach.

My mother was still in her mid-twenties then, bedazzling with youth and beauty and into her second of three marriages. She was not the mother to coddle a child, or cuddle, not that I would have stood still for such attentions; but hers was a presence that projected, a beauty that stopped conversations, and she was undoubtedly, irrevocably mine regardless her marital misadventures. Even at three I would sometimes cock my head and throw her an exasperated look. She would smile at my precociousness, sometimes frown, and never come to understand the sentiment behind the expression.

At twenty-three I was a father in a failing marriage. I remember the words I said, every one of them—every day. I remember my young son peering through his cracked door at the turbulence, the insecurity in his eyes. He is an adult now, laboring three time zones away and working to start his own family. I delved into that episode with him not long ago. He has no memory of it. Would I could be as fortunate.

At forty-three I could have remarried but didn't. I don't regret that in the least, but I still see her dampened eyes, so silently searching. I see the quiver in her cheek, and the stamina that held it all in check. I remember our first time together, our last time together, and every time in between. These are fond memories. Where she is today I cannot know, but she lives on with me just the same.

At sixty-three I finally came to understand it.

As my mother lay dying, and as my younger siblings jockeyed for primacy, I languished in torment. We were three siblings from three fathers, less siblings than free agents in orbit around our mother; but I was the eldest, also the only person still living who remembered her in those efflorescent days of her later youth. My siblings thought of her as old and frail and not in possession of her own wits. They had not inherited her steel, not an ounce of it. They only perceived what their idealized nostalgia would allow them.

Into our twenties, my friends and I were at last old enough to reminisce upon our earlier times together, helped along by bouts of beer-swilling that dimmed eyes and loosened tongues. They roamed widely through their memories, alighting upon some forgotten episode that they would suddenly recount with sloppy exuberance, as if they had just discovered a pearl in the muck while drunk. I would smile, or laugh, and act the expected part. I did not yet understand that they were experiencing something as if for a second time, while for me that time was a constant presence, all those memories aligned and ready for retrieval.

My mind is often crowded.

As an older child, I knew only that my mind was busy, always busy, in an endless repeat of those things I had seen and done, and which had left an imprint. Some of it was happy, some of it less so, but all of it made a deafening noise that followed me even into my dreams where, between the odd nightmare, my sleeping mind would simply recount the scenes I had lived so far. My friends perceived me as errantly peculiar, with a disquieting propensity to wander in and out of the moment. This was an eccentricity that I didn't recognize at the time and didn't know they sensed. I only knew that their behavior toward me was often odd, their friendships often fickle.

And weaving through all of this was the noise, the gaggle of accumulated voices, the reels that rolled relentlessly on, day and night, minute by minute, in and out of conversations and activities and admonishments by my teachers to pay attention. At the age of ten I discovered that I could make myself dizzy by twirling, and that during this state the noise would temper and allow room for other thoughts, for daydreams and imaginings and what I might do tomorrow. When coupled with long-playing music to drown out other sounds, I found that I could stretch my imagination into stories and characters that came as alive in my dizzied mind as the haunted memories they displaced. Those who saw me while this was going on thought I was learning to dance, nothing unusual about it.

My memory is not photographic. I am no savant. I do not remember every minor detail. Unlike those remarkable people with hyperthymesia, I cannot recall what I had for breakfast on a given date in years past, but I can recall many breakfasts over time, and with no idea whatsoever why those particular breakfasts left a lingering impression. I am eight and the breakfast is pancakes with maple syrup at a round linoleum table with yellow legs; seventeen and it's doughnuts and coffee in the school cafeteria; forty-one and it's chicken-fried steak and eggs at a rough-hewn bar;

this morning oatmeal with blueberries as the birds beyond my window puffed their feathers against the cold.

An abundance of research lays bare the fundamental fallibility of memory, especially in adolescents whose minds cannot yet define everything they perceive. My memory isn't perfect. I might recall a gift from one when it came from another, or a street sign on the right rather than the left. I will lose the lyrics to a song, misquote Shakespeare, and struggle to remember names. My memory, like everybody else's, is frail and prone to error, but without our memories, whether accurate, contrived, incorrect, or entirely misconceived, who are we?

I gained greater mental control as I grew into puberty and beyond. No longer distracted by the constant barrage, I made friends, made love, and made a living. Life seemed normal. And yet, as a sociopath instinctively learns to hide his true nature, I learned to revel in nostalgia when others reveled, to laugh or commiserate when it seemed appropriate, even though the subject of that revelry had never once slipped from the forefront of my mind. I still couldn't define the difference between myself and others—I wasn't even consciously aware that there was a difference—but I adapted just the same.

The chemotherapy savaged my mother. I had been abroad when the decision was made, out of contact and unaware until the course had been unequivocally set. I would have argued against chemotherapy if I had been present, and I expect my argument would have carried, because with it would have come clear recollections of what had been, prescient predictions of what would come, and a reminder that mortality will meet us all. Well into her eighties, there was no chance that noxious chemicals would extend her life, but would instead render what days remained to her a misery. All she'd needed was someone to hold her hand and say it.

When I finally got back and was able to see her, she was shrunken, bald and gray, a shocking portrait and the worst manifestation of my fears. My mother was built for poise and purpose, not for this. Barely a generation removed from the hardscrabble times of her mountain kinfolk, she had once stood stoically against violence and heartache and heart-rending loss. But despite this steel legacy, the idea of death had always terrified her. She kept that eventuality bound tightly in denial, as if she might yet slip through her years with her dignity intact, never forced to face that fateful day.

She broke down when she saw me, shuddering sobs that shook her wasted shoulders. She cried not from the pain the drugs had induced, but the pain of her pitiful condition in eyes she knew remembered her as she had once been. My mind raced through those memories, smoky eyes and noble cheeks, bituminous hair in a shoulder flip, glossy full lips, and glamorous in high heels. Then the later years, age encroaching, changes of hair color and style but the back always straight and the shoulders high, what she had lived to be, not what she had been reduced to now.

"Bear up, Mom," I said almost reproachfully. "Remember who you are and where you come from."

"Keith! Don't talk to her like that."

That's my name, Keith, and that scolding voice came from my sister Leena, only three years younger but my memories during those three years separates us as if they were a lifetime. Also present and brooding was my little brother, Jarrard. At fourteen years younger, I thought of him more as a cousin than a sibling. He had been a disagreeable kid and had become a loathsome adult. Outwardly indifferent to us, and as equally uninterested in the greater family history, I had begun referring to him in my mind as *Footnote*.

I live a thousand miles north and east of my old hometown, in a quiet hollow between timeless hills in the region where my mother was born. My mother's husband, Zachary, always beat a hasty retreat when I came to visit. We weren't close and never had been. I was a first son from a first marriage, a relic from his wife's past that he couldn't reconcile, as if he could only maintain a necessary fiction in my absence. This created a clumsy tension between us that nobody else ever noticed, and was one of the reasons I preferred to live so far away. Still, he undoubtedly loved my mother. He treated her well, endured her vanity and made her happy, although I could wish that he understood her the way I did. If he had, perhaps he could have stopped her from going through with the chemo.

It was while meeting my sister's indignant brown eyes after her rebuke that I caught the first tingling hint of understanding. Zachary and

Jarrard were late arrivals, an unavoidable accommodation, but Leena was old enough to remember nearly as much as I. How could she have allowed this to happen? Unless...unless she couldn't see the way I saw, as if her perception were stranded in the present. Could it be possible that she didn't recognize that our mother lived in a self-image that reached all the way back to a petted youth, of a startlingly self-possessed young girl who blazed from black and white photos of austere country folk just emerging from their most trying times since the Civil War? No image of that girl failed to grab one's attention, whether the background be a grainy class photo, a family portrait, or a throng of country kids. Stripped of that image, she would die sooner rather than later.

Death doesn't frighten me, nor does the idea of it. Death is an inevitability. I have known this since I was six, when my mother uncomfortably explained it to me, albeit cushioned with heaven and angels and such, and probably as much for her benefit as mine. Since then I have lost more than my share, through the attrition of living as well as lives. This hasn't hardened me, although I now know that with my dry way of dealing with loss, those closest to me presumed it had. For most of them, memories fade. For me, each of those lost lives reside within easy reach, always, preserved as if in amber.

I mulled this as I made my long journey home, leaving my mother as well as she would ever be again. My memories reeled through the dark of night, through the decades, punctuated by the headlights coming the other way. When you're finally old enough, the cycles become as obvious as painful joints, circles large and small joining into chains that link with one another until they form a net that catches us all. I now knew with a jolt that this is what I saw that my sister and others didn't, how events sixty, or a hundred, or a thousand years ago could still resonate today. This was the difference my memories made real, a perception of deep time that nobody else in my circle of family and friends had ever conceived let alone mastered.

It's not easy to put into words, to describe in ways that don't sound cold and detached. Loss was still loss, although moderated with pragmatic certainty. My mother's death would be sad, but it would not be tragic. She'd had a long life; she'd outlived her entire line. She was the last of her generation and of those who had come before her. The only tragedy was the way she would now have to bear that end.

My sister called me soon after I got home.

"Mama's back in the hospital," she said. I winced. Mom did not like being called Mama, which made her sound older than she wanted to accept, but she wouldn't upbraid a daughter who bruised easily and still complained about a traumatic childhood that I knew firsthand was far from the case. "You need to come back right away," she added with a few drips of opprobrium. In her mind, I should have taken up residence down there until the matter resolved itself.

"I can't. She'll be okay. She's tougher than you think."

"But the doctors say this could be it." Her voice was rising in panicked pitches.

"The same doctors who gave her the poison?"

"You weren't here! You don't know anything about it."

I exhaled to give the tension time to disperse. We all juggled eggs when we dealt with Leena, all except Jarrard, whose narcissistic vision never ventured beyond his own self-interest. The two were perpetually at war. I kept my distance from them because I didn't need the additional clutter. As for Leena, though, at one misplaced word she would cry havoc and let slip the dogs of self-righteous indignation, and from that point forward would become as approachable as a cactus.

She hadn't always been this way. I could still see her as a little girl, gentle, vulnerable, and as withdrawn as a wounded bird needing protection, which I offered as well as I could until she grew a little older and began to compete against me for our mother's affection, something I neither competed for nor ever doubted. What I pushed back against was her annoying meddling, her need to diminish me in our mother's eyes. Sibling rivalries are as natural as nature itself. Neither of us was immune to it, if not obvious at the time, at least obvious to me now. Over a period of perhaps five years, an eternity to a child, I was unkind to Leena a total of four times. These are four episodes I can recall clearly, comprising behaviors of which I am not proud, for which I make no excuses, but which represent nothing today beyond the cruelties children are capable of committing upon one another. Despite this paucity of persecution, she magnified each into a self-sustaining myth of martyrdom that she maintains to this day.

It is tedious.

"You're right," I said, choosing my words carefully. "But Mom's tough. This is because of the chemo, not the cancer. I'll be there when it's time."

She hung up abruptly, just a breath away from summoning that self-righteous indignation of hers. I could have tried to explain it to her, but with her linear mind she would never have understood, not the way I had come to understand ever since my latent epiphany. I knew if I went down there it would provoke an irreparable schism that would drive home the last nail, something else to add to our mother's woes.

I had talked about this with my mother some years back, after her brother died, leaving her the last of her line. The day would come, I told her. Had she made plans? She tried to evade the topic but, my stomach fluttering uneasily, I kept at her until she had nowhere else to retreat. I was stunned to discover that she hadn't made a will.

"You have to, Mom," I said vehemently if not queasily. "I have a will, you should too. There's nothing morbid about it."

"That's not something I need to think about right now."

She was up into her seventies by then, but still carried herself with grace. This talk had rattled her. She fled the room on the pretext of a chore, leaving me alone with Zachary. He looked at me reprovingly, as if I had purposefully upended the fragile foundation of his cobbled reality, and yet not daring to rebuke me while my mother held sway.

"I love your mother," he said pleadingly, as if he needed to convince me. "I don't know what I'd do without her."

Her own husband didn't have the courage to broach the topic, neither did Leena or Jarrard, so it fell to me, and damn if that didn't make me furious.

I wrangled Mom back into the room. Zachary had left us, too uncomfortable to participate. "Mom, listen," I said. Her nose was a little red, and I gulped miserably. "I know what you want, the *do-not-resuscitate* and all that."

Her father—my grandfather, whose rheumy blue eyes and country wisdom have never strayed far from my thoughts—had drowned slowly from the fluid in his coal-damaged lungs while my mother and I could only sit helplessly by. The doctors revived him over and again to face the same strangling agony, until at last he regained enough fortitude to refuse any further heroic efforts. This had traumatized my mother (me as well), and she had vowed it would never happen to her. She'd made me promise, and now I was trying to keep that promise.

"If it happens," I went on, purposely choosing *if* rather than *when*, "Leena and Jarrard will turn against me. I won't be able to do anything about it."

"They wouldn't do that," she responded indignantly, although her expression revealed otherwise.

Soon thereafter she filed a living will, and the weight fell off me. Her wishes would now be honored by law, and I wouldn't have to destroy the family to see them through.

Days later, Mom made it home from the hospital as I had predicted. Leena called me twice more over the next three weeks, each time proclaiming with absolute conviction that our mother's end was imminent. Leena proclaimed this in a voice caustic with recrimination, as if she had been appointed the arbiter of matters between my mother and me. Why wouldn't I come, she would ask. Why can't she see it for herself, I would ask myself.

My mother survived these bouts as well, as I had known she would, but that did not mollify my sister.

The weeks went into winter. Gray day in and darker day out, my memories were a tangle of torment. I saw my mother in pearls in '61, in gold in '81, and in something hand-made that the grandkids had given her in 2001. There she was in her white Mustang in '65, preening proudly at the onlookers who gaped at the novel new car, the first in our town; stately in her white Cadillac in '82, having at last arrived at success; and comfortably ensconced in her (also white) SUV recently, large enough to accommodate her oxygen cylinders along with her groceries. I called her between her bouts of pneumonia, as often as she could speak. She was always stoic on the phone, as if protecting me from the extent of her suffering. Leena and Jarrard saw it first-hand, though, and spared no opportunity to spear me with guilt.

I wasn't avoiding my mother's condition. I wanted, desperately, to take my mother away from that place and return her to her family's mountains, where she could regain her color and her dignity and live these last years or months to her best. But that's not the way my siblings would see it. For them, our mother must be pandered to, pampered, her vices accommodated, her life extended regardless the cost, while for me our mother must not be allowed to feel sorry for herself, to let herself go, to give up. Her lungs were liquid, her body too weak to sit erect for any period of time, but it was the loss of her dignity that would ultimately kill her, and they couldn't see it, or else they couldn't accept it. No steel. That gene had passed them by.

I have lived alone for more than thirty years. This is the life I prefer, although I never understood why until my recent revelation. The crowding only gets worse with age, and quiet is the only balm. But—with my own spurt of indignation—none of them had ever been alone for more than a few days at a time in their lives! They had no idea the challenges I faced, the complicated arrangements necessary for even a short time away, or the anguish I experienced in solitude while they gathered round with their extended families, commiserating and sipping wine.

I weakened, to my disgust. My sister's provocations had finally begun to encroach upon my resolve. Now when I spoke with my mother I found myself pathetically fishing for validation, well aware of what I was doing and how unseemly it was but I couldn't help myself. As adults we're supposed to put these childish impulses behind us, but how can I when that childhood is never not present in my mind? I only needed one word, the simplest confirmation of understanding. That word never came, leaving me with only the steel for comfort.

The coming of spring seemed to revive her, although the rattle in her voice belied that. We spoke of gardens and flowers and painting projects. She envied my vitality.

In an instant I was six and saw her in white shorts, shirttails tied at her waist and her hair pinned up as she knelt to her garden, Leena toddling about as if dazed by the outdoors. My mother loved to garden. She loved to paint. These were themes in her life that carried on until the day she accepted that first noxious injection. Her gardens at her home with Zachary had been praised, her roses, her dahlias, her poinsettias, but now they wilted. She had only recently repainted her living room for the third or fourth time. Whenever I came to visit, I was first taken on a tour of the new paint, the new crafts, the new art on the walls. She needed change, the only way she could temper her restlessness, her way of forestalling another misadventure.

Sometimes Zachary would answer the phone when I called. "Hey, Zach—"

"Just a minute." Then I would hear him holler, "Honey? Keith's on the phone."

He was always abrupt with me that way, as if I might never want to speak with him directly. When I could hold him on the line, to ask how he was doing or how it was going, he would only scroll through my mother's condition in a monotone and then holler her to the phone. He never called when my mother had a spell, but instead delegated this to Leena, whose judgmental memorandums I could have done without, but without which I would know nothing at all. The idea of Jarrard shoring up these communications was laughable.

She crashed in the late spring, was taken to the hospital, returned home, crashed again, returned home, and then crashed again in a cycle with no apparent end—three days home, a night in the hospital, three more days home, another night in the hospital... When I spoke with her, she was weak but resolute. What was the problem, I asked. What were the doctors doing? She didn't know.

She didn't know.

I called Jarrard, if only for a break from Leena. Jarrard didn't know. I called Leena. She had been staying at the hospital with Mom, but she didn't know either. I sighed and gazed out the window at my gardens, buzzing with pollinators and blazing with color. It was time to act.

The arrangements were hasty but they would do. I drove fifteen hours, arrived stiff, sore, and limping. I needed a whisky first. Mom was back in the hospital. She smiled weakly when I went in, under a thin institutional blanket that did nothing to comfort the emaciated body beneath. Zachary was there, asleep in a chair.

"Hi, Mom," I said with a dry swallow.

"Hey," she patted the bed weakly. "Come sit."

I sat and took her hand, warm but skeletal. I had no words. Neither did she. Equipment hummed and pumped. The curtains were open. It was a brilliant, warm day outside, but cloying and cold in the room. I shivered. "Can I get you anything?" I asked.

She shook her head. "No."

A side table was cluttered with medicine bottles: steroids, antibiotics, potassium, blood thinners, and much else that I couldn't identify. I scanned her monitor. Her vitals weren't bad, considering. "Are they helping you?" I asked. She shrugged.

Zachary roused, saw me and seemed startled. "Keith."

"Zachary."

"When did you get in?"

"Just now. What are they doing for her?"

"We don't know."

That last statement was too much. "I'll be back," I said tersely.

I prowled the corridors until I cornered one of the several doctors assigned to my mother. He seemed nervous, in a hurry to move on. He wouldn't meet my eyes. He assured me, though, that my mother would be released soon. "Why?" I asked, and he had no answer.

I appealed to an approachable nurse, who appealed up the line until we found a doctor who was willing to listen. "My mother is readmitted every few days," I told him. "I don't want you to release her again until she's stable."

"That makes sense," he said. I thought I would explode.

It was pulmonary edema, misdiagnosed at least once as pneumonia. They would ply her with antibiotics, drain her lungs and send her home, only to see her back in a few days when her lungs filled again. I saw my grandfather, lying there choking, and thought I would be sick. I had promised. I had promised.

They kept her two more days at my intense insistence, days in which she regained some color and strength. I brought her Mexican food for lunch, and begged her to go for healthier fare in the future.

"Why?" she asked fatally.

"Because your cancer is one thing, not everything. It's slow-growing, it hasn't metastasized, and if you look after yourself you'll feel better and stronger." I said this with conviction, hoping that with improvement I might lure her home with me. "And lay off the wine," I added, not quite scolding.

"A little wine won't hurt me."

"A little wine can interfere with your medications, and after the chemo your liver is weak. Just stay off it. Please?"

"Okay," she nodded grayly.

I knew this would be a challenge for her. My mother loved wine as much as gardening and painting. A memory pushed its way in. My mother was dolled up and on the arm of Leena's father, making light banter on their way out for an evening on the town. Kennedy was president then. My mother was ebullient. "And one of them asked me," she said gaily, "will that be red wine or white wine?" Leena's father chuckled. My mother, raised in a small Appalachian town, was still in her impressionable twenties at the time, young enough to be flattered by such a seemingly sophisticated question.

We brought her home after three days in the hospital, stabilized and even with a little blush in her cheeks. She was scheduled to have a tube put in so that she could drain her lungs at home. She was looking as well as she could under the circumstances. With healthier living, I thought, she might even regain some of her vitality. Her garden needed work, I reminded her as a nudge, but she didn't seem to have the will to respond.

Leena lived a few hours away and had gone home. Jarrard was doing whatever it was that Jarrard did. I offered to cook that night, something new and healthy that I thought they would like. Zachary was still too befuddled from the ordeal to object. Mom just nodded her assent.

I got to work in the kitchen as the sun went down, peeling sweet potatoes and chopping garlic. Zachary was elsewhere, and Mom was dozing under a blanket on her couch. The news was on. I wasn't paying attention, and then the doorbell rang and it was Jarrard.

He walked in imperiously, offering me barely a nod. Zachary appeared as if called to stand his mark, and then father and son went to huddle with Mom on the couch. I continued in the kitchen, sipping a whisky as Jarrard held forth loudly on escapades that escaped me completely. And then he came into the kitchen, shouldered past me, poured a glass of wine, and carried it to my mother.

"I thought we agreed, Mom," I said, feeling betrayed.

"A little wine won't hurt her," Jarrard countered with pique.

"Just a little," Mom added, already looking tipsy from a single sip.

"I have some food coming," Jarrard said to Mom then.

Mom brightened. "Oh, really? What?"

"Mexican food. Your favorite."

I threw everything in the sink, and then retreated to a corner stool with my whisky while Jarrard plied my mother with wine and Zachary beamed his approval.

"I'm sorry I couldn't see you in the hospital," Jarrard told her as she sipped, her hand unsteady and her face already flushed. I ground my teeth.

"I had them keep her there longer," I interjected into their tipsy scene. "They kept sending her home when she wasn't stable."

"So you think you know more than the doctors?" he asked with undisguised disregard.

"I know enough to not bring her home when she can't breathe."

Mom was by now dizzy from the wine, Zachary was patently looking elsewhere, and it was all I could do not to punch Jarrard in the face.

This went on well past the news hour, Jarrard monopolizing the moment while I sipped bitter whisky. The food was delivered and they gorged, and then Jarrard—finally—got up to leave. I followed him into the dark.

"She needs to get off the wine and the fatty food," I told him point blank. He had just opened his car door but now slammed it.

"Who do you think you are? Don't be comin' down here and tellin' us what to do!"

He was in his late forties, misshapen with testosterone injections, HGH, and overzealous weightlifting, while I was in my early sixties, excellent cardio but low muscle mass. If I'd been ten years younger I would have given him the beating of his life. "I'm the oldest," I said instead, slapping my chest for emphasis.

"You're not the oldest in *my* family," he spat back.

I regarded him with disgust. "Man, there's something wrong with you."

He moved forward threateningly. "*Me?* There's nothing wrong with me. You're the one hiding out while your mother's in there dying."

"I'm not hiding out," I said with surprising calm, thinking that we were all dying, it was only a matter of when.

"I don't care what you're doing!" he erupted. "I want you out of my life. I don't want to see you again. Don't call me, don't contact me, just leave!"

He spun around and screeched away. Zachary watched all of this from the window, with no thought to intercede. Outnumbered, I could do nothing. I left the next morning.

Summer was long and hot, and my mother's tone shifted subtly. She seemed impatient now when I called, short on commentary and in no way prepared to challenge her youngest. "You could straighten it out between Jarrard and me, Mom," I told her. "I know we're all adults, but you're still the parent. Just put your foot down."

"I love all of my children equally," she said.

"Of course you do, but you know how Jarrard is. Zachary won't do it, it has to be you."

"Oh, Keith—I can't face that right now."

I understood where she was coming from. Jarrard's temper frightened her. One misplaced word might send Leena into paroxysms, but Jarrard elevated even that. Anger him and she might never see him again, might never see her grandchildren again. He was that petty.

And so my worst fear had been realized, the reason I had stayed away. Leena offered no consolation when she called me.

"Mom's down again."

"How bad?"

"Bad enough. They've moved her to hospice. You should come."

Her voice was completely uninflected, just a statement of facts, her dispassionate tone revealing more than she knew.

"I can't," I said, squeezing my eyes.

"Why not?" An edge of hardness limned her voice now.

"Because of Zachary and Jarrard."

"I wouldn't let anybody keep me from seeing *my* mother when she was dying."

"That's easy for you to say, you're not the oldest and you're not a son."

"What does that have to do with anything?"

It was so simply obvious that I couldn't believe she didn't see it. Literature was full of this kind of thing; movies were full of it—how could she possibly be so oblivious?

"Do you know what a palace coup is, little sister?" I asked in equal amounts of disgust and despair.

"What are you *talking* about?"

"Zachary and Jarrard have their own little family with Mom, and that family only holds up if I'm not in it."

"What? Are you kidding me?"

I went on explaining as if her tone hadn't gone sarcastic. "This was always going to happen, Leena. Mom didn't think so, but I always knew it would. You see, if I'm not around then Jarrard is the only son. He has his dad and his mom and the grandkids, and all with the same last name. Do you understand?"

She sighed in exasperation. "I think you're just making excuses. They've been married for fifty years, for God's sake."

"Actually, forty-eight years—"

And then my memory tore off to Christmas when I was twenty-eight. I had come down to be with the family, or rather, to be with my mother. Zachary was no less aloof than he had ever been or would ever be, Jarrard was almost fourteen and not improving with age, and Leena was off starting a family in another state.

I noticed an uncomfortable tension the moment I walked through the door the night of Christmas Eve. Zachary fled as he always did, but this time without even a perfunctory greeting. Jarrard was wound up and surly, snapping at Mom and ignoring me completely. Mom smiled only faintly at my arrival, a departure from her usual effusive welcome. She did come in for the hug, which was tentative, and then I definitely knew something was off.

"What's going on?" I asked her in concern.

She shook her head tightly. "Nothing."

Christmas Day was no less tense. Christmas dinner was dry, tasteless, and silent. I gave serious thought to going off and getting a hotel room somewhere, which I nixed when Mom came out with the pecan pie and made an effort, albeit futile, to lighten the mood. I went to bed early that night to escape the biting glances among the three of them, as if they were passing hurtful notes to one another.

The father/son duo slept late the next morning. I poured myself a coffee, then found my mother on the screened porch, quietly sipping her own coffee as the gray morning rose around us. She still smoked back then. A cigarette burned lazily in her ashtray.

"What's going on?" I asked her, taking a seat and looking over my shoulder to make sure none of the windows were open.

She tightened her lips and stared at her coffee, and then said bluntly, "I'm going to divorce him."

My head reeled. "Why?"

"I don't want to talk about it."

"You are talking about it."

She fixed eyes on me. "You know what I mean."

I raised my cup to hide my discomfort. In truth, I could have gone to the end of my life happy not to have had Zachary and Jarrard in it, but they *were* in it and Mom was fifty now. How many more times could she do this and not wake up one morning old and alone?

"You're upset about this, aren't you?" she asked flatly.

"I'm upset for you," I said.

"I thought you would be happy about it."

"I might've been once, but that was a long time ago." I wanted her to take the hint without me having to say it, that she was getting too old for another misadventure, but that hint was too oblique for her to notice.

She reached for her cigarette, took a nervous pull then said, "I can't live with him anymore."

"I'm not sure you can live without him."

"I promise you I can," she said testily, baring the steel, and I knew right then that she wasn't simply venting, she was really going to do it, she was going to divorce him, and then what?

"Look," I said, almost a plead, "you and Zachary have been married for fourteen years. You were only with my father for two years and Leena's father for three. You've lasted this long, so why can't you work it out?"

She looked away and puffed at her cigarette. "You don't understand, Keith," she said, exhaling smoke into the gray.

"No, Mom, I don't, but if you get divorced, what are you going to do? Get married again? What if that doesn't work out either? And really—" she looked at me now with hard eyes, "—do you seriously want to handle Jarrard by yourself?"

She snorted and smiled tragically. "Jarrard can be sweet sometimes."

"I've never seen it."

"You're too much older, Keith. You don't really know him."

"I know enough." She threw me a sympathetic look. "Just wait it out, Mom. *Please.*"

"We'll see," was all she would concede.

They stayed together, and by all indications, overcame whatever differences they'd had. Their lives seemed happy. There was devotion. Even Jarrard settled down for a while. Mom and I never spoke of this again, nor did I ever mention it to Leena. It's another memory now, a memory that never leaves me.

"—but that doesn't matter," I continued with my sister. "If I go down there it'll all blow up, and Mom doesn't need that right now."

"Mom needs *you.*"

"Mom has me and she knows it."

That ended our call but not the conflict. I tried to reach Mom, but Zachary was running interference now. I tried again the next day and got through. Mom was lucid. She sounded exceptionally present considering the dire prognosis Leena had given me.

"Hi Mom. How are you?"

"I'm doing better," she said.

"Leena left me with the impression that you weren't doing well." I softened this from, *Leena left me with the impression that you were at death's door.* Leena had clearly magnified the situation to make me feel guilty.

"Oh, I'm in hospice care now. That only means there aren't any more treatment options, that's all. I feel fine, and I'm going to come see you when the leaves turn. It's always so pretty up there."

My stomach clenched. Mom would never be strong enough to come up here again. She knew it and I knew it, which meant she was trying to ease it for me. My lips trembled and I stifled a sob.

"I can't be there, Mom."

"I know, honey."

"I'm so sorry."

"I know."

"I wish you could be here. I want you here so much." A sob escaped.

"I wish I could be there, too. Have you visited your grandmother's grave lately?"

"I *was* there not too long ago."

"And Daddy's, too."

"Yeah," I sniffed, "Grandpa's, too."

"I'm glad you're up there with them."

"I want *you* up here with them."

"I know, honey, but that can't happen. You know that."

"I know—" I had to stop as the sobs wracked me. "Damn, Mom— you know to me you're still twenty-five."

She chuckled wanly. "I'm a lot older than that now."

"We're all a lot older, but that's how I see you. That's how I'll always see you."

"And you're just a little boy always getting into trouble."

"I *was* always getting into trouble," I laughed and cried at the same time. "Do you remember when I was four and ate that toadstool?"

"I can't believe you remember that."

"Yeah, my friend next door—his name was Julio, I remember—he said his dad planted them and they were good to eat. So I ate one. It tasted awful. Pungent, you know? Like sour dirt. But we kids were al- ways eating fruit from the trees and such, so it didn't seem wrong at all. Then that little blond haired girl from across the street came over. I don't remember her name, but she was pretty, I remember that. She said they were poisonous, so I got scared and ran in to tell you, and then I don't remember anything after that."

"You were in a coma. We thought you were going to die."

"Huh. Well, the toadstool didn't kill me, but the hornets almost did. Do you remember? It was when I was exploring when I was five. They stung me all over my head, and I swole up so bad that I couldn't open my eyes."

"I remember," she said, breathy now.

"And you sat with me—days, I think—and dabbed that oatmeal on my face."

"That's all the medicine we had back in those days."

"And it hurt, too, but I was never scared because you were with me and I knew I would be okay. And then that time when I was seven and stepped on that rusty nail—"

"Honey, I can't believe you remember all of this! You didn't tell me about it. I didn't find out until I saw the scar on your foot, and then I was terrified you'd come down with tetanus."

"I'm sorry I put you through all of that, Mom."

"It wasn't your fault." Her voice shook and she swallowed. "Honey, was I a bad mother?"

I tried to hold back but I couldn't. The tears came in a flood and my throat felt constricted. It hurt to swallow and I couldn't steady my voice. "No, Mama. Why would you think that?"

"Leena said something."

"Still?"

Damn you Leena, I thought. With her stilted memory, she could only remember her emotions, magnified as if through a lens, while I saw the reality of those times.

My memory raced again, Thanksgiving when I was thirty-five. Mom had tears in her eyes when I came to the door. Zachary was absent, of course, and Jarrard hadn't come down from school that year. Leena was living close by at that time, but was having Thanksgiving dinner at her house.

"What's wrong, Mom?" I asked, distressed.

"It's nothing." She wiped her nose and made a pained smile. "Just stuff."

She looked as if she needed to get away, so I talked her into a road trip the next day. We drove to the beach. Mom loved the sea. The sky was gray enough to drive away the holiday crowds, but it wasn't too cold. We walked the beach as gulls dived into the slate waves.

"Was I a bad mother?" she asked into the brisk wind.

"What?" I was stunned. "Why would you say that?"

"Leena came over yesterday before you got here..."

She trailed off at that, needing to explain no further.

"No, Mom. You're a great mother."

"Do you really mean that?"

"Of course I do. I mean—we were never hungry. We always had a place to live. And we were loved—"

"Your sister doesn't think so."

"My sister doesn't remember anything. I do."

Mom felt much better by the time we got back home, and I'd hoped that would be the end of it. But obviously it wasn't.

"Mom," I said, back in the present and struggling to control my voice. "I wouldn't be who I am if it weren't for you, and I wouldn't want to be anyone else."

"I know you really mean that."

"I do, Mom. The others could never love you the way I do. Sure, they love you in their own ways, but they don't see you the way I do. They can't because they weren't there."

"Those were different times."

"Those were the best times."

She was getting too weak to continue, so we rang off. I promised to call her the next day, but couldn't get through when I tried. She died later that night.

Leena called me in her judgmental monotone. "Mom died last night," she said.

"Shit."

I had felt listless all day, gray beyond the windows. Somehow, I had known.

"Did she suffer?" I asked in a sob.

"No. She died peacefully in her sleep."

"Thank God," I breathed in relief. Mom was so afraid that she might suffer the way her father had. I don't think Leena, who had never spent much time with our grandfather, was aware of this at all.

"Someone will call you about the funeral," she said no less judgmentally, and then she hung up.

Mom wanted to be cremated, her ashes scattered at sea. It was the only way she could weave that line between her disparate families and offend no one. I wanted her here, Zachary and Jarrard would have wanted her there, and I had no idea what Leena would have wanted.

I didn't go down for the service. If she had been buried with a stone I would have gone down to pay my respects and seek what solace I could, but bumping elbows with Jarrard and Zachary while they laid claim to her urn and her legacy would have only marred the day. Instead I visited her parents, I visited her childhood home, and I spoke some words, but most of all I remembered—I remembered everything.

Time is fluid until that inevitable day, streams of possibilities that venture into new seasons of memory; and then time becomes immutable, caught between those seasons until the last person forgets. That day will come for all of us. No optimism in the future, in technology, or in one's deity will belay that fact. I only ask: When that day comes for me, what will I remember?

ABOUT THE AUTHOR

Kirk Ward Robinson was born and raised in south Texas, and has since lived in every continental American time zone. He is an inveterate hiker and cyclist who prefers to travel and explore the world that way. His wide-ranging career has included roles as a chief operating officer, bookstore manager, stagehand, bicycle mechanic, and executive director of an educational non-profit organization in cooperation with the National Park Service. Robinson has been twice named to Kirkus Reviews' *Best Books*: in 2012 for *Life in Continuum*, and in 2015 for *The Appalachian*. He earned five stars from Foreword Clarion Reviews for his novel *The Latter Half of Inglorious Years*.

These days he maintains a small ancestral farm in the hills of Tennessee.

www.kirkwardrobinson.com

www.ingramcontent.com/pod-product-compliance
Lightning Source LLC
Chambersburg PA
CBHW021701110726
47902CB00007B/2021